# TAPPING THAT ASSET

## A TEMPERANCE FALLS ROMANCE

### LONDON HALE

# LONDON HALE

LONDON HALE

*To Brighton.*
*Becuase you never read these anyway. Stay sparkly!*

# chapter one

AJ

WHEN A WOMAN told me in no uncertain terms she was down to fuck, who was I to say no? Especially when that woman could hold an intelligent conversation with me for hours *and* make me laugh several times during it. Did it matter that I'd met her just hours before? That I only knew her as Kennedy—no last name, no personal details? No, it sure as fuck did not. Not when she was my every wet dream come to life—thick, dark hair I planned to have wrapped around my fist by the end of the night, cocktease lips that were lush and supple under mine, and legs that looked a mile long in that short as hell skirt she wore.

What dumbass would say no to that? Not this one.

"Jesus, Kennedy." I groaned into her mouth, pressing her against the door to her hotel room as she locked her legs around my waist and ground against me. The heat of her pussy reached my cock even through the layers separating us, and the thought of sinking inside that heaven nearly brought me to my knees.

Later. I could get on my knees later. Right now, I needed to fuck her.

From the second she'd walked into the Marina Grand Hotel's bar, I'd wanted her. Hadn't been able to think about anything but what noises she'd make when she came. I'd had no intention of doing anything but work when I'd stopped in to check out what specials the small but highly frequented tourist trap had on tap this month. Checking out my competition now definitely didn't mean what it had to me just a few short years ago when I'd played in the majors. And as much as I loved baseball, I'd take sampling different beers over poring over game tapes any day.

As we were a new brewery, it was important to stay on top of the trends. And while the locals were Pops' Hops bread and butter, that didn't mean we ignored the huge tourist market on Temperance Falls, which had meant a few hours at the fanciest hotel on the island. After a long day at the brewery, I'd had plans of sampling a few of the new offerings, then heading home to get in some intimate time with my right hand, too tired to put in more effort than that to get laid.

And then she'd walked in.

Walked in and promptly sucked all the air from the room while drawing the eye of every single person in the bar. Tits high and full, skirt showing off miles of smooth legs punctuated by heels I wanted digging into my shoulders while I sank inside her. Stunning and captivating, she'd had no problem holding her own during our conversation, hadn't been afraid to challenge me at every turn, which was hot as fuck. She held herself in a way that said she was probably born into money…and that she was used to people noticing when she walked into a room. She had a commanding presence she practically dared you to ignore.

I sure as hell couldn't ignore it.

"Want you." She delivered the words straight between my lips while she tugged at the back of my T-shirt, attempting to yank it off.

"Thank fuck, because otherwise, this would've been awkward."

Her breathy laugh was cut off as I pinned her to the door with my hips and grabbed my shirt by the back of the neck, pulling it off and tossing it somewhere behind me. Desperate to feel her hands on me.

She didn't disappoint. With a hum of satisfaction, she ran her fingertips over my shoulders, down my arms and chest. And as much as I loved the feel of her fingers on me, I needed to do the same to her. Wanted to feel her and taste her. I tugged down the front of her tank top, taking the cups of her black lace bra with it. *Christ*, her tits were perfection, the soft, pink tips begging for my tongue. Who was I to deny them? With a groan, I sucked one nipple into my mouth, pulling deeper the louder her moans grew, the harder her fingers tightened in my hair.

I blew a sharp gust of air against the wet tip, flicking my eyes up to her face. "You like that, don't you? Like my mouth on these perfect little tits."

She answered in another moan, yanking on my hair and guiding me back down to her breasts. I couldn't remember the last time I was this hard, my cock throbbing behind my fly, trying to bust through the zipper. All from a little foreplay—her breathy groans in my ear as I sucked her nipples, her hips undulating against me, pressing down on my cock, and those nails—*fuck*. With a shudder from her on a particularly deep pull of my mouth, she scored her nails down my pecs, no doubt leaving an angry trail of red marks in her wake.

I groaned, pulling away from her as I glanced down at the damage she'd done. My cock twitched at the sight of those lines on my skin. At the thought of me driving this composed woman out of her mind. I looked up at her, stared into those half-lidded hazel eyes, a thrill shooting through me at the pure want written on her face. "You trying to mark me, pretty girl?"

"You said you'd be mine for the night. I'm just staking my claim." She leaned forward, nipping my bottom lip. "Don't worry. The only marks I'll leave on your cock will come from my lipstick."

Christ on a goddamn cracker, how did this

woman already know exactly what to say to make me throb with want, to make my cock weep as it strained to get closer to her?

"I hope you didn't have any plans for the foreseeable future, because they're officially canceled." I trailed my nose across her collarbone, traced the swells of her tits with my tongue. "It's going to take me hours to do everything I want to this body. And when I'm done, you'll be so hoarse from screaming, you won't be able to talk."

"Don't make promises you can't keep, sport."

A laugh rumbled from my chest, rusty and low. "Don't worry, baby. Before the night is done, you're going to lose count of how many times you've come. *That* is a promise."

I squeezed her ass then slid my hand between her legs from behind, groaning as damp panties met my fingers. "Jesus, you're wet."

She rocked against me, trying to direct my hand exactly where she wanted it. "Have been since I walked into the bar and saw you. Are you going to keep me waiting?"

Much as I wanted to feel her come on my fingers and my tongue, those would have to wait. Especially when she looked three seconds away from exploding in my arms. I wanted to feel that on my cock, wanted her riding it when she fell apart.

"You saying you need my cock, pretty girl?"

"Pretty sure me asking you to come to my room should have cleared that up, but in case I'm wrong…"

She nuzzled my neck, lifting her mouth to allow her lips to brush my ear. "I want your cock, AJ. Stop teasing me."

Part of me wanted to keep taunting her until we both were driven halfway out of our minds. But the heat from her pussy was like a fucking beacon, the warm wetness that greeted my fingers as I pushed her panties to the side and felt her smoothness for the first time enough to make *me* beg.

"This is just to get the edge off before we start the real show," I said as I pressed her into the door and fumbled with my fly. "Gonna make you come all over my cock right here against the door where anyone walking by could hear." I pulled out my aching cock, ran the head through her slit, both of us groaning at the contact.

"AJ," she moaned, head tossed back as she tried to pull me closer.

With a shuddering breath, I rested my forehead against her neck, the quickness of her breaths against my skin reassurance this crazy connection wasn't one-sided.

I licked a path up her neck, fluttering my tongue at her pulse point. "Later, I'm going to spend an hour just eating your pussy. Make you come half a dozen times all over my tongue." I tugged my wallet out of my pocket, plucked a condom from inside, and rolled it down the length of my cock. "Then I'm going to lie back and have you ride me so I can watch those perfect tits bounce. Feel you come all over me again, even when you swear you don't have another one in you."

"Promises, promises." With a groan, she rotated her hips against me, trying futilely to get me inside her. "You should use that mouth for something more than just words."

"Oh, I plan to." I held her panties aside with one hand and gripped my cock with the other, running the head through where she was soft and warm and so fucking wet for me. I scraped my teeth along her jaw, reveled in the indentations her nails made on my back, in the quick *pant pant pant* of her breaths against my ear. "But first, I need to feel what this pussy is like."

And then I thrust deep. A slow glide of my cock into the tight fist of her pussy. Back and forth, until I'd worked my whole length inside. Until we were finally flush. Until I was balls deep in the heaven that was her pussy.

"Fuck. *Fuck*." I gripped her ass, held her tight to me as I throbbed and twitched inside her, my cock begging me to forget everything and jackhammer away until I came deep inside. "Knew it. Knew this pussy'd feel like heaven."

Head thrown back, she rocked against me. "More. I need more."

"Not just more, pretty girl. *All* of it." I pulled back and snapped my hips forward, taking up a fast, frenzied rhythm. She clung to me, her arms tight around my shoulders, her nails digging into my skin.

And I loved it. I fucking loved that she'd leave those marks on me. That I'd wake up tomorrow and have a physical reminder of an amazing night with a woman I certainly hadn't planned for.

Gripping her ass with one hand, I brought the other between us, seeking her swollen clit with my thumb. On the first brush, she shuddered in my arms, whimpering against my ear. When I ran soft circles all over her slit, her pussy fluttered around my driving cock. But when I focused my efforts, my thumb flicking back and forth against her clit in quick, unrelenting strokes, she went off. Head tossed back, she ground down on me, taking me inside as far as she could while she groaned through her release.

"Shit, pretty girl." I continued rubbing her until she went boneless in my arms. Until she rested her head on my shoulder, her fingers brushing over where her nails had marked me, her hips a slow, steady roll against me. Like she couldn't get enough. Like, even after coming so hard the people across the hall no doubt heard it, she wanted more. Needed more.

I pushed away from the door and swung around toward the paperwork-covered dining table. Shoving the files out of the way, I laid her out in front of me, my cock still deep inside her. Still begging for its own release.

Grabbing her ankle, I propped it on my shoulder, groaning as I slid even deeper. Loving that I had her spread out for my eyes and my hands and my mouth. Loving that we were just getting started.

"Now that that first orgasm is out of the way," I said as I pushed deep, rotating my hips and pressing against her clit, "it's time for some fun."

# chapter two



THE ACHE BETWEEN my legs pulled me from sleep, a reminder of the long night I'd enjoyed. A night filled with wine, laughs, and lots of orgasms. The best kind of night. I stretched, almost wishing AJ were still next to me to go for another round. Okay, more than almost. I definitely wished he were still there to tease me awake with his fingers and talented lips. The man had made me see stars.

He'd also left before dawn as I'd asked him to. I had no time for morning awkwardness or the lies people told one another. "Call me," "See you around," "We should do this again sometime." No thanks. I'd never been one of those girls. Though it had been a lot harder to kick AJ out than any man before. Difficult, but needed. Something I'd never had trouble with before.

Rolling out of bed, I shuffled my way into the bathroom, needing to clear my head. Shower, coffee, then work. My routine. My life, sad as it was.

The warm water did nothing to quell my aches or quiet my mind. No man had ever snagged my attention so quickly or so completely. But AJ was… different. Charming, kind, funny. He was the type of man you set your claws into and hung on to. The type of man you wanted to be yours for more than one night. I wasn't staying on Temperance Falls for long, though. Just a week or so for work, then I'd be headed back to New York or wherever else my older brother had found some small, privately owned brewery to put out of business.

I really wish he'd get off his craft beer kick.

I was applying my lipstick when my phone rang for the first time of the day. Shit, that meant Charles— my stubborn, arrogant, workaholic brother—had called at least two times. Do not disturb mode could only work so well.

I counted to five before swiping to answer. "Yes, Charles."

"Why haven't you been answering my calls?"

*Don't let him get to you so early.* I pouted a kiss at the mirror, admiring the perfect red pucker I'd painted on. Wondering if AJ had been able to wash off the kiss marks I'd left all over his body yet. I'd made sure the ones on his cock had been exceptionally dark, and he hadn't complained a bit. "I was just finishing getting ready. Should we meet in the restaurant downstairs?"

"Don't bother. I have coffee and pastries in my room. Be here in five." With that, he ended the call, and I could only sigh. Two minutes. It took Charles exactly two minutes to destroy my post-sex buzz.

I took a deep breath and squared my shoulders. There was nothing I could do about my brother's attitude, only my own. It was time to get to work. Charles would want a full rundown on where we stood with the budgets of each project currently in motion, and seeing as how I was the CFO of the family business, he'd be expecting that from me. Plus more.

It was the *more* that was the issue.

If I could stick with numbers—with finances and formulas and statistical probabilities of return—I'd be happy. If I could get back to running an actual restaurant instead of our corporation, I'd be fucking thrilled. I hated all the travel he expected of me, hated how Charles dragged me from location to location across the Midwest because he wanted to see the damage he was doing in real time. I didn't have the same drive as Charles, the same need for conquering he did. I just liked math and food; they made sense.

I'd grown up in a family restaurant my mom ran, and I'd loved every second of it. Had been happy to work beside her right up until the day she died and take over her duties as needed. Handling the payroll, purchasing, and revenue had been where I'd found my love for finances, which my dad had convinced me was a more practical college major instead of heading to culinary school as I'd wanted. A thousand times, he'd said to me, *"Don't be the cook, Kennedy, be the owner."* Those words had stuck.

Whatever he'd said to my brother had instead made him obsessed with being the best in all the wrong ways. The need to own more, build higher, and shutter smaller businesses along the way? That was all Charles seemed to focus on, and it'd never sat well with me.

Technically, Charles was my boss, though. So I'd fly from state to state with him whenever he told me to, and I'd go over every detail of every budget until he was satisfied we weren't spending a penny more than he wanted us to. I could daydream about a small restaurant and a quiet life another day.

And I could remember last night's lover later… when I had time to maybe track him down to see if he had any more nights open while I was in town.

———

"It's too much."

I fought to hold back my growl, growing more and more irritated with my brother with every refusal. We hadn't even secured the land for the Temperance Falls project, and he was already throwing up roadblocks about our next purchase planned for a suburb in Illinois.

"Charles, the town only rezoned the property last

month, and the price reflects that change. If you want that particular location, we'll have to pay the higher cost."

But Charles was nothing if not stubborn. "No. It's too much. Find a different plot of land."

I sighed as the driver pulled into the parking lot of Pops' Hops, the local brewery we were about to put out of business. The last thing I wanted after six hours of arguing over every fucking dime was watching my brother's ego grow as he compared the small restaurant to the 125,000-square foot behemoths we built, but he'd demanded I come along. At that point in the day, I wasn't even daydreaming about tracking down AJ for another night in my bed. Instead, I was dreaming of a warm bath, a bottle of wine, and for my brother to fall into the lake surrounding the tiny island we were staying on. Was that too much to ask?

"Hurry up, Kennedy." Charles rushed out of the car the second it stopped, looking far too excited. "I bet they only have a fifteen-barrel system in there. What's that? A thousand barrels a year? Amateurs."

"It's 2,250." I grabbed my purse and shaded my eyes at the building before me. Tall and slightly rustic, it held a charm that was unmistakable and perfect for the little island. Our ridiculous, modern monstrosity would leave everything around the building in shadows, would stick out like a sore thumb in such a quaint island town. Yet this place almost seemed as if it had been grown instead of built. It looked natural and made for the space it inhabited. In other words, it was the perfect balance of building and land. I loved it on sight and hated my brother for not seeing the damage he was about to do.

Speaking of my brother, he looked confused. "Two thousand…what?"

I shrugged, following Charles through the lot filled with more cars than I would have expected for the time of day. "Fifteen barrels times three brews per week times fifty weeks per year assuming a standard two-week shutdown is 2,250 barrels yearly production. Depending on pint-to-barrel sales, as well as breakdown of ale to lager, of course."

Charles shot a frown my way as he opened the door. "Yeah, whatever. Ours will be better."

For the thousandth time in just the past month, I wished my parents had given him a little less attention as a child. That had to be where this immature, needy little streak to be "the best" came from. And we, as a company, weren't the best. We were a solid player in chain restaurants—medium- to high-end Italian fare being our bread and butter. We had that model locked down, and I would go up against anyone in the same space in a competition to see who was best. Breweries and brewpubs were new to us, but Charles had gotten a bug up his ass about them last year, so we'd spent months expanding into that market. That expansion had been slow and rough with a steep learning curve we weren't quite over yet, and the profit margin was too small for the amount of time and energy each location required. If it were up to me, I'd cut our losses and look at something more on-trend like farm-to-table concepts or healthier quick-service restaurants. But Charles got his way like always, so beer it was.

Inside Pops' Hops, the noise in the dining area carried a social, happy tone to it. Tables were filled across half the space, people talking, eating, and drinking away their late afternoons. The overall vibe of the place was close to a sports bar, but just a little nicer, and it showed in the number of female clientele taking up seats at tables and the bar. That was a great sign. The owners were definitely doing something right.

The hostess seated us in a booth along the windows, handing us the menus before drawing our attention to the phenomenal view of the woods with a peek of the lake over the trees. Jesus, this location was ideal.

"It's a nice brewpub," I commented, years of working in restaurant operations making me look at all the options a little differently than most people would. "The menu's well-balanced and original. I bet they turn a nice profit on food."

"The real money's in the tanks."

I wanted to argue that point, but my brother wasn't paying attention to me. Instead, Charles smiled as the waitress approached, raising his hand to make sure he had her attention.

"Hey, sweetheart. What's your most popular beer?"

God, someday a waitress was going to take his

patronizing sweetheart and shove it up his ass. I know I would have.

But the young lady simply smiled. "This time of year, it's the summer Pilsner. We actually make a mean shandy out of it with a local lemon soda if you're interested."

"I prefer my beer straight," Charles said, making me want to roll my eyes. The man rarely drank beer at all. "Two Pilsners please, and is the owner around, by chance?"

I kicked Charles under the table, knowing exactly what he was about to do, but he ignored me.

The waitress suddenly looked a little worried. "Um, one is, but the other's not in today."

"Could you send him over when he's free? I'd like to talk to him about the business."

"Sure." She glanced my way. "Any appetizers to go with those beers?"

I handed her the menu, wishing I could apologize for my brother. "No, thank you. Just the drinks."

"Of course, and I'll bring Mr. Phelps over."

Charles chuckled as she hurried away. "How could a Pilsner be their most popular? That makes no sense. And a shandy? Please. The girl must not know a thing about the business."

"Can you not do this?" I hissed, leaning closer. Wishing for once he'd listen to me. "For your information, shandies have risen eight percent in popularity over the past year, with continued growth expected. This place may just be ahead of the curve. And for God's sake, stop calling women sweetheart."

"It's a term of endearment."

"It's degrading."

Charles sighed loud and long. "Here we go. You gonna climb back onto your feminist high horse today? Because I'm not in the mood."

*And that was the moment I killed him, Your Honor.*

But I had no time to think about all the ways I wanted to maim my brother because the waitress was back, two large glasses of golden brew on her tray. "Two Pilsners, and Mr. Phelps said he'd be over in a few minutes. He's on a call."

"Thank you," I said, accepting my drink. Wondering if I could give Charles a concussion with it if I tossed it at his head. I figured it would need more mass to get the right velocity, so I didn't throw it.

Wish I would have gotten a beer that came in a big, glass stein instead.

As soon as the waitress left, I took a sip of the golden liquid, licking my lips afterward. "Wow."

"What?" Charles glanced my way, frowning.

"I can see why this is the most popular beer." I went back for another taste, nearly sighing in delight. It was bright and not too hoppy, nicely rounded without the sting of bitterness I usually expected. Wine was my drink of choice, but I could enjoy a good beer, and this was definitely a good beer. "It's like summer in a bottle. I bet that shandy made of this is superpopular."

Charles chugged from his glass, nodding as he slowed down. "It's not too bad, I guess. Make a note to find out who their brewmaster is. We might want to snag him once this place closes."

And back to that subject we went. "Charles, we don't need to open a brewery here. There's already a fine-dining Italian restaurant, but there's a missing pocket on the island for casual fare. Something like our—"

"No." His answer left no room for argument. "The land is too big for our other restaurants. We need a large footprint, which means brewery."

"We could find another parcel, a smaller one. Stay well under budget."

"We'll stay under no matter what. That's why I pay you the big bucks."

"But there's no wiggle room this time—the real estate is already at the top of our price range. If anything goes wrong with the deal—"

"So make sure nothing goes wrong." He took another long drink of his beer, nodding as he put the glass down. "The outlets at the mall revamp site are too small, and that Main Street they have is too kitschy for the direction of the company, which leaves us few options here. I want the tourist dollars this place represents. That corner lot you found is perfect, so you're going to get it for us. Yes, it's at the top of the budget, but top doesn't mean over. We'll come in in the black."

I wanted to argue more, to try to persuade him to look at other options no matter how futile that would be, but someone walked up to our table and stole all my attention. Someone with dark hair and a smile that could melt the panties off a nun.

Someone who probably had my scratch marks and lipstick stains still decorating his body.

"I understand someone's looking for the owner of Pops' Hops," AJ said, just before his eyes met mine. Recognition flashed across his too-handsome face, and something warm unfurled inside of me. Something that made me want to lick my lips and lean a little closer to him. To see if he still smelled like lemon and man.

But before I could say anything, before AJ could do more than smile at me, Charles opened his mouth.

"Yes, I was. I'm Charles Rochester, CEO of Rochester Entertainment, and my company's building a new brewery in town." Charles' grin turned wolfish as AJ whipped his head around to stare at him. "I wanted to meet the fool I was about to put out of business."

# chapter three

AJ

THE LAST THING I'd expected to see today at Pops' was my hot as fuck one-night stand. When I'd left Kennedy—regrettably—in the early hours of the morning before we'd had a chance to go for yet another round, I'd figured that was it. I'd never see her again, no matter how badly I wanted to. She was on the island for only a few days because of business, so that was that.

Except now she sat in our handcrafted mahogany booths my best friend and co-owner Luke and I had spent hours deciding on, some douchebag at her side who was, evidently, dead set on putting Pops' Hops out of business. And man, the guy had a set of balls on him. Who went into a place of business and threatened its owner like that?

Apparently, the kind of guy Kennedy attached herself to.

"Well, Charles," I said, putting as much false sincerity into my voice as possible, "so nice of you to come and introduce yourself. And this is…?" I turned and looked at Kennedy, pretending I'd never met her before. Trying to figure out their story. Was this arrogant asshat her boyfriend? She didn't wear a wedding ring, but that meant fuck all. Shit, he could be her *husband*.

And even though I'd known from the start that our…whatever it was…was only going to be a one-night thing, I couldn't stop the jealousy that swept through me, fierce and fast.

I fucking hated the thought of her being someone else's.

She cocked her head, eyes questioning. "Kennedy Rochester. Charles is my—"

"My sister isn't important here," the asshat interrupted, "as anything other than the CFO of Rochester Entertainment. You might want to focus your attention on me as I'm the one who's built eight breweries in the past year and put almost twice that many out of business."

The relief was swift but short-lived. The guy was a jackass of epic proportions, sure. But he wasn't *her* jackass. The woman I hadn't been able to get out of my head wasn't anyone else's. But she *was* part of a family who apparently reveled in crushing small, locally owned businesses. Had done so to more than a dozen, and that was only in the past year. Those facts didn't make sense, didn't add up with what I knew of her from our conversation last night.

But then, anyone could lie for a few hours, especially when sex was the end game. And what a gloriously spectacular end game it had been.

Charles droned on, his voice like nails on a chalkboard, but I couldn't look away from Kennedy, couldn't even make sense of the words the dickbag spoke. All I could do was stare into those gorgeous hazel eyes and remember her face as she'd ridden me, lips parted in pleasure, hands braced on my chest as she'd shuddered and shaken over me. As she came for the ninth time—hell yeah, I'd kept count.

I could name every single one of them—two was on the dining table; five, she'd been reclining in the chair, my tongue buried deep inside her; eight had been by her own fingers while she'd sucked my cock, leaving a ring of red around the base—and I had plans to recall them at a moment's notice for the foreseeable future.

By the way Kennedy bit her lip as she stared at me, her cheeks flushing, the thoughts were written all over my face.

"Do you even understand what I'm saying to you, Mr. Phelps?"

I dragged my eyes away from Kennedy, meeting Charles' irate expression with a bored one of my own, though I felt anything but. This cocknugget was threatening my livelihood, but I'd be damned if I let him know he was getting to me. "Oh, I understand. I'm just fresh out of fucks to give."

His nostrils flared, his face turning an unnatural

shade of red, which pleased me to a ridiculous degree. "I would expect a business owner to act a little more professionally."

Cocking my head, I stared down at him, loving that the position we were in put me at an advantage as I towered over him. I thought this guy could use a little beating down. "And professional to you is coming into a place of business and threatening its owner?"

"I consider that a courtesy. I figure small-timers like you and your business partner would want to take advantage of the advanced notice that you'll need to find a new source of income since I'll be taking this one."

I barked out a laugh. He might have put a shit-ton of other breweries out of business, but he obviously hadn't done his research on Temperance Falls. Of course, the kind of family mentality we had for our residents wasn't something you could find via a simple Google search. It was something you had to experience firsthand. "Hey, if you think you can come to this tight-knit island community and go up against two guys who've lived here their whole lives, be my guest. It's your money."

"Yes, I guess it is." Charles stood, and I got a sort of smug satisfaction that he wasn't tall enough to be eye level. He reached into his pocket and pulled out a business card, pinching it between two fingers as he held it out to me. "Nice Pilsner. When you're laying people off, tell your brewmaster to come see me."

I glanced down at the card, then very deliberately

crossed my arms over my chest without taking it. "My brewmaster will say the same thing as I do: fuck off."

He scowled, then tossed the card and some cash on the table before spinning on the heels of his too-expensive loafers. "Let's go, Kennedy."

I turned to her, paying no mind to her tantrum-throwing brother. Last night, she hadn't seemed to recognize me—as a former MBLer or as the co-owner of Pops' Hops. That was the tiny spark of hope I had. Because otherwise… If she'd known I was a partner in Pops' Hops and she'd slept with me? I blinked the thoughts away, then came right out and asked because I wasn't one for playing games. "Did you know?"

She stared at me for a moment, then gave a soft, subtle shake of her head. "I knew my brother's plans, of course. That they involved you? No. I wouldn't have…pursued you if I had."

I braced my hands on the table and leaned toward her, my eyes flicking down to those full lips painted the same red she'd left on my cock. "There was no acting last night, pretty girl. That was one-hundred percent you."

She stood, stepping close and crowding me. "You're right, and for what it's worth, I woke up hoping to track you down so we could spend more time together. I'm sorry this business deal will prevent that." With a quick brush of her hand across my hip, she slipped past me toward the door. "It really is a great Pilsner. I'm impressed."

"Of all the things I've shown you in the past

twenty-four hours, I'd think the Pilsner would be the least impressive."

She shot a grin over her shoulder, her ass swaying distractingly as she walked away. "I'd have to agree with you on that."

———

An hour later, I'd dug up everything I could find on Rochester Entertainment. They had two hundred restaurants and were estimated to employ more than four thousand people. It wasn't just a family business—it was a goddamn empire worth millions. They were extremely good at what they did, despite Charles being a soul-sucking asshole. Which led me to a single conclusion: we were fucked.

Yes, Temperance Falls residents protected their own—lifers or transplants alike. If you called the island your home, you were one of us. So our neighbors and friends and family would sooner drink piss than have some of Rochester Entertainment's shitty beer. But the tourists? The ones who didn't know any better? Who had no idea about the history of each building, about the layers of family that went into each business? The ones who made up a solid forty percent of our income? They wouldn't give a single shit.

"All right, I'm here," Luke said, blowing into the office, irritation written all over his face. Anything that got in the way of his nights off with his girlfriend

Hannah turned him into a grumpy old bastard in three seconds flat. "What's so important it couldn't wait until tomorrow?"

"Sit down."

His brows shot up. "Seriously?"

When I only answered him with an unwavering stare, he dropped onto the small leather couch against the side wall. "Well? What's the emergency?"

I blew out a breath, took off my baseball hat, and scrubbed a hand through my hair before replacing the cap. "We had a couple visitors today. The CEO and CFO of Rochester Entertainment stopped by to try our brew."

"Never heard of 'em."

"They're a family-run conglomerate out of New York with more than two hundred restaurants under their name, eight of which are breweries."

"Okay," he said, stretching out the word. "I'm still not following. They want to partner with us or something?"

I barked a humorless laugh. "Not quite. They want to put us out of business."

"What?"

Bracing my elbows on the desk, I leaned forward. "Their plans, from what I can gather, are to build something here, take business from us, and leave us floundering."

Luke's knuckles turned white as he gripped the couch's armrest. "The locals would never go to them over us."

"The locals, no. But the tourists?" I shook my head, turning the laptop around to face him. The screen showed a plot of land for sale farther inland than our own. "The only land big enough to house their kind of monstrosities would be the old farm stand north of Main Street. With that prime location, tourists wouldn't care that our building's been here for over a hundred years. That the bar was handcrafted by Jackson, the original floors restored by Big John. Shit, they wouldn't even care that our beer's better. They wouldn't even *see* us over these assholes."

Luke stared at me for a moment, jaw clenched. "*Fuck*."

"Yeah, fuck."

"We just started operating in the black last year. We don't have enough saved up to take a hit like this. We—" Luke growled and pushed off from the couch before pacing around the small office, hands in hair. "What the fuck are we gonna do, AJ? We can't... *I* can't..."

He didn't have to finish the sentences. I already knew what he was going to say. Had been the only thing I could think about from the moment that smarmy asshole had opened his goddamn mouth. Luke had put his life savings into this place, brushing me aside when I'd offered to front the entire start-up cost. What the hell else did I have to spend my money on?

Despite only playing in the majors for less than a season, I'd been compensated well. *Beyond* well. My signing bonus had been obscene, not to mention my first year's salary. So, yeah, *I* didn't need this, but Luke sure as shit did.

Besides the monetary aspect of it, this was his life. Our brew recipes had been passed down from his late stepfather. What we did here meant something to Luke. And thus, it meant something to me.

"I'll take care of it." I closed the laptop and stood.

"How the hell are you planning to do that? You think they're going to back down just because you ask nicely? Shit doesn't work like that, man."

No, it didn't. Not with a man like Charles. He was an arrogant asshole who thought about one thing and one thing only: money. No amount of pleading with him would change that. Kennedy, however…

"I have an idea, but I need to head out. Can you cover tonight?"

He was already nodding before I got the words out. "I'm not sure your charm is going to get us out of this one, but I sure as fuck hope it does."

Me too.

# *chapter four*

KENNEDY

OTHER THAN MY attraction to a business owner we'd soon put out of a job, I couldn't work through what it was about this particular build that bothered me so. This was what Rochester Entertainment did. We researched real estate, demographics, and local food options, picked a format that fit the market, and built a restaurant. Easy. Virtually plug and play after all the years we'd been in business and all the concepts we'd developed. It wasn't anything I stayed up at night thinking about even when I knew other peoples' financial futures were on the line. Yes, we put other restaurants out of business at times, but usually, they were already failing.

Pops' Hops wasn't failing, but it would be vulnerable to a second brewery moving in to the area. Especially one with a corporate base as large as ours. We could afford to take a loss for a year or so. Charles would complain, but the long-term profits would cover it, as would our established restaurants. I hated knowing that charming, perfect place with the unique menu and delicious beer would be forced out because of us. I hated knowing AJ would fail at something not because of his doing, but mine.

And he would fail. Charles wouldn't give up until ours was the only brewery on the island. His ego wouldn't let it go. But Charles didn't have the same heart and soul in a business that AJ had. I could feel it when I walked into Pops' Hops—could practically smell it. AJ and his partner loved that place, they poured everything they had into it. Though, from just the one night together, I knew AJ wasn't the type of man to do anything half-assed. A great lover, a great businessman, charming as all fuck, and handsome as sin? The man was exactly what most women wanted.

Even me.

"Never happening, Kennedy." I shook my head, trying to clear my scattered thoughts, but it was no use. I was toast. It was time to unplug for the night. To have dinner and perhaps a glass of wine.

Or seven.

I grabbed the room phone and hit the three buttons I'd become well acquainted with since arriving on the island.

"Room service."

"Yes, I'd like my standard dinner and a bottle of Pinot Noir, please."

"Of course, Ms. Rochester. Claude will be up shortly."

"Thank you." And thank God for good hotels with amazing chefs in the kitchen and a courteous room service staff. I wasn't in the mood to mingle downstairs.

Stretching, I headed into the bathroom. I needed a shower to clean off the residual stink of the day. And maybe let my mind wander to the reasons why my muscles were still sore even so many hours after my tryst with AJ. Maybe.

As if I could stop those memories from bombarding me.

I was clean, dressed, ridiculously aroused from the fingerprint bruises AJ had left on my thighs, and pulling my hair up into a bun when a knock sounded. I tied my robe around my waist and headed for the door, grabbing my wallet along the way so I could tip Claude for saving my life with wine and a charcuterie tray.

"I hope you got your lavender honey shipment today. I missed it the other night," I said as I opened the door, finally snagging the ten-dollar bill I was looking for.

"Unfortunately, the only honey I had today was very early this morning."

Oh hell. I'd know that smooth voice anywhere. Of course, he showed up here. That was totally my luck. I raised my head to look into his green eyes— so bright, so pretty—and deep inside me, something began to burn. Something hot and needy. Something I knew AJ wouldn't be up for satisfying. There was no way he was here for a repeat of last night, no matter how much I wished it were true.

It was obviously fight night in my hotel room instead.

Before I could respond, Claude appeared at his side. "Good evening, Ms. Rochester. I have your dinner."

"Uh…thank you, Claude. You can set it on the table, please."

"Of course." Claude nodded as he passed me, but I barely noticed. My eyes stayed locked with AJ's. The two of us stood in the open doorway, staring, not saying a word as Claude arranged the plate and opened the wine. Everything I wanted to say to the man before me tumbled through my head. Things like "I'll make it right" and "My brother's an asshole, but he'll see the light" and "I'll find a way to stop him from building here," but they were all lies. I couldn't lie to AJ…or to myself.

"Will there be anything else?" Claude asked as he finally stepped out into the hall.

"No, thank you." I handed him the ten and waited for him to disappear before addressing the man who had monopolized most of my thoughts all day. "It's been a shit day, and I plan on being wine-drunk in about ten minutes. Care to join me?"

AJ followed me inside, shutting the door behind him with a quiet snick. "I'm more of a beer guy. Though you know that by now."

I hummed, doing my best to hide the flinch the harshness of his tone caused. He had the right to be pissed. Hell, I was pissed, and Charles wasn't fucking with my business.

Ignoring the pain lancing my chest, I headed for the minibar. "I've only got a couple of Stellas and a Bass Ale. Nothing like the Pilsner you're brewing."

"I'm not here for a drink, Kennedy."

Of course not. "Yes, well… I have a feeling I'm going to need one for this."

I poured two glasses of wine and handed one to AJ before leaning a hip against the desk and facing him full on. Jesus, he was just so…much. Tall, fit, gorgeous. All handsome and yet somehow pretty. The man's face should have been on advertisements for something—women would buy whatever he was selling without a second thought.

AJ cocked his head a little, squared his shoulders, and set down his still-full wineglass, looking so damn sexy as he prepared to go to battle with me.

"I need you to tell your brother to back off of a Temperance Falls build."

One bottle was not going to be enough wine.

I drained my glass and poured another. "I can't. Charles is like a bulldog when he decides what he wants. Slobbery and completely single-minded."

"The woman I met last night didn't seem like the type to utter the words 'I can't.'"

"Yeah, well, the only thing I can't ever seem to handle is my brother." I took another sip before setting the glass down so I could slather two pieces of hard cheese with the lavender honey. One for me, one for AJ. "I can tell you and your partner have put a ton of time and thought into Pops' Hops. The place is amazing in more ways than I can articulate—it outshines the cookie-cutter breweries my brother designs in every detail."

"Then why are you going through with it?" He waved me off when I held out the honey-coated cheese for him. "Why can't you go find some other place and put one of your monstrosities there instead?"

"Don't you think I would if I could? Hell, I've tried. I've run property comps and market analysis and population density reports until my fingers bled. My opinion doesn't matter. Charles is set on Temperance Falls and refuses to listen to me when I tell him a different style of restaurant would be a better fit. He wants his brewery, and he wants it here. Nothing will sway him." I took another swig of wine, shaking my head as I swallowed. "Not even his own CFO giving him forecasts that would scare off any other company in our position."

AJ paced from one end of the room to the other, looking more and more frustrated with each pass. "He won't ever get the locals' business. It'll be one hundred percent tourists, and while that's a solid chunk of revenue, it's nowhere near what a place like yours needs to operate in the black. He'd be a fool to open here."

"Oh, he's no fool. He's a heartless businessman

with an ego the size of Manhattan and a refusal to look at numbers strategically, but not a fool." More wine. I needed so much more wine. "AJ, I know how much you've put into Pops' Hops. If my brother had half a heart that wasn't decomposing underneath all his money and pride, I'd make that case a thousand times over. I'd beg and plead on my knees for him to make any other choice."

He spun in my direction, his glare pinning me in place. "I don't give a shit what *I've* put into it. I have more money than I know what to do with. But my best friend and partner? He's sunk everything he has into this. It's the only thing he has left of his father. And I won't let it fail."

Aw, man. This just got even more complicated. I knew about AJ's baseball days—he'd told me all about the injury that had ended his career far too early—but not about his business partner. Friendships in business were hard to keep strong, a fact we'd learned early enough when my dad's business thrived and some of his friends' didn't. So we'd be costing AJ not just his business but likely also his friendship. Wonderful.

I set my glass down, stepping right in front of AJ. Forcing him to stop…really, really close to me. "He doesn't do sentimental, AJ. He won't care about any of it. He'd build a brewery right next to yours and sell all the beer for a dime a pint just to crush you. It's not our business that fuels him—it's ones like yours. He loves the kill. He wants to see everything you've put into your restaurant splattered across the parking lot."

"He sounds like a real stand-up guy." AJ inched closer, making me want to retreat...or pull him closer. His eyes were dark and angry, a muscle in his jaw twitching and giving away how hard he had to be clenching it. He was so close, so worked up. I wanted to tell him I'd figure it out, that I'd solve the problem, but I couldn't. I wanted to appease him so he could bend down and kiss my lips the same way he had last night, but there was no way.

"I'm sorry." My voice sounded weak, the crushing pain in my chest a feeling I'd never dealt with. An ache for a loss of something I never really had. "I wish there were more I could do, but he won't listen. The only thing he cares about is budgets and winning. He's heartless."

AJ shook his head, obviously thinking something over. When he looked back up at me, when his eyes met mine with a hungry expression on his face, I knew I was in trouble.

"Selfishness obviously doesn't run in the family." He stepped into me, my hips sliding onto the desktop on instinct, my legs spreading for him out of pure want. "Because you were anything but last night, weren't you? Greedy as hell, but not selfish."

Playing with my attraction to him was not fair. Not fair at all...but something I couldn't resist. I grabbed him by the belt loop, pulling him closer, letting my robe fall open. Every moment of the night before came back to me in a flash—his smile when he first approached me, how he made me laugh at the bar, the way we'd inched closer as the night wore on. The first kiss—so strong, so passionate. The multiple orgasms as he'd fucked me on every surface in this hotel room.

But this time was different—this time, there was a swirl of anger between us. Of pain. The man wasn't going to be gentle with me. A thought that only made my body burn brighter. Hotter.

AJ held my gaze, his eyes growing darker, his breathing too fast. He had to feel the same draw, remember the same moments. Hell, he'd bent me over this desk last night and pounded into me from behind. And now, hours later, here we were again, though with a little conflict in the way. There was no more understanding, no agreement between us on what this was or when it ended. There was only desire, tension, and that lingering sting of temper.

The room seemed to grow warmer, the attraction between us making our breaths come faster. I kept my eyes on his, kept him as close to me as he'd allow. I'd never wanted someone to break, to snap the thread of control holding them back, so much. Never wished for a man to take control and demand reparations from my body the way I did with AJ.

The way I knew I never would again with another man.

"AJ, I—"

"I shouldn't be here. Not with the sister of the man putting us out of business."

"Please." I refused to let him go, pulling him

closer. Nearly crying when he pressed his hips against mine. "I know how bad this is, I really do. I wish there were more that I could do to help. I wish…" I sighed, my shoulders curling. Surrendering. "I wish you were here for a repeat of last night."

AJ dropped his gaze, his jaw clenching harder as he took me in. And yes, it may have been shameless, but I leaned back just a bit, let my robe fall over my shoulder an extra few inches. Made sure my legs were spread enough so he could catch a glimpse between my thighs. And I knew he did. I could feel how hard he was against me. This attraction definitely wasn't one-sided.

He licked his lips, sliding his eyes up my body, past my exposed breast. "I don't think you'd want me right now, pretty girl. I'm mad as hell."

Fuck it. Time for a Hail Mary pass. I hooked my knee around his hip, running my toes up the back of his leg. "Mad doesn't scare me. Never again feeling what I did last night does."

"Mad means you're not going to get what you had last night. No fun orgasms. No flirty stares over your shoulder while you ride my cock backward. Just pure, raw fucking." He leaned over me, forcing me back as he ran his hand up my inner thigh. Teasing me with his fingers so close to where I wanted them. "I might even make you beg."

A shiver racked my body followed by a surge of pride that was unavoidable. Beg? Hell no. I didn't beg for anything. "I'd love to see you try."

With a growl, he attacked my pussy. There was no other word for it. Using his body to push me back until my shoulders hit the wall behind the desk, he thrust two fingers deep inside me and pressed his thumb against my clit in a way that was so rough, so hard. So fucking perfect. My entire body arched into his touch, the pleasure of it worth the sting. Having any part of him inside me again worth the crash I knew would come tomorrow.

But at least I had this night.

"AJ." I grabbed his shoulders, wanting more contact, wishing to feel his skin against mine. Needing to take advantage of every second we had.

"You ready to beg yet?"

When I shook my head, he tore open my robe the rest of the way. Exposing me completely. The view was so wrong, so dirty—him fully dressed, me basically naked, his hand buried between my legs. And the sounds. There was no denying I was already wet for him. Hell, I'd grown wet just thinking about him earlier. Positively filthy.

And he wasn't done with me.

Dipping down, he pulled one nipple into his mouth, sucking hard as his hand kept working me. Kept pushing me toward a cliff I needed to fall over. Every feeling built inside, swirling through as each nerve ending began to quiver. To quake. As my orgasm came closer and closer.

But AJ had a point to make. When I was so close, when I was grasping him by the hair and chanting *yes* over and over again, he pulled away. He actually let me go.

The bastard simply stopped.

"What are you—"

"What did I say about begging? If you want me to make you come, that's all you have to do." His smile turned wicked, his eyebrows raised in what looked like a challenge. "Come on, baby, I want to hear it."

"You're kidding."

He smirked then pressed on my clit again, making my entire body jump at the abrasion against my sensitive flesh. "You think I'd kid about feeling your pussy come around my fingers?"

He waited, his face so close to mine, panting just like I was. There was no denying he was aroused—his cock sat hard and heavy against my thigh even through his jeans—but he wasn't surrendering. And as I stared, as I practically gaped at him, something inside of me shifted. Gave me the strength to let go. To trust this man, no matter how angry he was. No matter how rough. He'd never hurt me.

Not like I was going to hurt him.

"Please, AJ." I rocked my hips, seeking his hand again. "Please."

But he held back. Didn't give me what I needed. Instead, he ran his nose along my jaw slowly, teasingly, nipping at my ear before whispering, "That was pretty weak, considering the kinds of orgasms I give you. You remember them, don't you? Was your throat sore this morning from how much I made you scream?"

"AJ," I groaned, grabbing him by the neck and pulling him to me. Crashing our lips together in a fierce kiss that nearly sent me over that edge I was chasing. Nearly, but not quite. "Please, I want you."

"We don't always get what we want, pretty girl." His words were harsh, but he didn't stop. Instead, he licked down to my breast, teasing my nipple with his tongue and teeth. "Is that as good as you can do?"

Not even close. "I want you. I need you. Please, AJ. Please don't hold back." I pulled his mouth to mine again, biting his bottom lip just to prove I would. "I'm fucking begging you."

A smile crept up his handsome face, his body softening as it lay against mine. "There are those magic words."

And then his hand was back, fingers seated deep inside me. Pressing against places that made me see stars. His thumb flicked back and forth over my clit, making me gasp and cry out his name. But it was when he bit me, when he set his teeth against my neck and pressed down until I jerked from the pain of it, that I came. Long and hard, shaking all over, I screamed his name as my entire body locked down in my orgasm.

AJ pushed me through it, keeping his fingers busy, making sure I got every ounce of pleasure from his touch. And when I was done, when I'd practically collapsed against the desk, he finally pulled himself from between my legs.

"Love how you look when you come. Though I

much prefer seeing it while my cock's buried inside you." He brought his hand to his mouth, licking the fingers that were still wet with me, making me quake all over again at how filthy he was. "So fucking sweet. Maybe I'll give you my tongue later. If you ask nicely."

Later. God, I loved that word. And though I wouldn't tell him so, I knew…I'd beg this man all night if he let me. So I reached for him, pulling him in for another deep kiss. Moaning as I tasted myself on his tongue. Smiling against his mouth as he bucked his hips when I grabbed his cock through his pants.

"Make me beg for it."

# chapter five

AJ

HAD ANY OTHER woman in history had the power to undo me like this one? Jesus Christ, all Kennedy had to do was look my way with her fuck-me eyes, and I was a goner. Even though she'd done the begging, I might as well have been the one on my knees.

It was some kind of cosmic joke that she could undo me like this but was also the very definition of off-limits. In my twenty-eight years, I'd never before experienced something like this—the instantaneous connection and off-the-charts chemistry that went further than mere attraction.

And it wasn't one-sided. Couldn't possibly be.

Even though she'd been reluctant to utter those breathy pleas, she'd done it. Had looked right into my eyes while she'd clung to me, hips wild as she rode my fingers and begged me over and over. She'd softened. For *me*. Something I was nearly certain she didn't do as a rule.

"I think we've already established I won't have a problem making you beg, pretty girl." I slipped my arm around her back and tugged her forward. Didn't stop until she had her legs wrapped around me, right where I wanted them. I turned toward the mattress and tossed her on it, her tits bouncing distractingly with the movement. "You *do* remember what I did to you last night, right?"

She tipped her chin in agreement. "Impossible to forget."

I stood at the side of the bed, looking down at her. Hard as fucking steel behind my zipper. Desperate to feel her, but I couldn't. Not yet. "I won't make you beg yet, but if you want my cock, you need to come over here and get it."

She stared up at me for a moment, thoughts flashing like neon signs behind her eyes. Then she rolled to her side before getting up on her hands and knees and crawling toward me. Jesus fucking Christ. My cock twitched behind the denim, the way she smiled up at me proving she knew exactly what she was doing.

Once she was close enough for me to feel her warm breath through my jeans, she stopped. Reached out. Traced a torturous path down my achingly hard length. "I'm here. Now what? Tell me what you want me to do."

"Take it out," I said, my voice raspy and raw. Tired of the teasing, yet wanting so much more of it. "Take it out and then wrap those lips around my cock and suck me deep."

"So damn bossy." But she did as I told her, undoing my button and zipper before shoving my jeans and boxer briefs down over my hips. My cock sprang up, heavy and so fucking hard, leaking from the tip. Reaching for her, throbbing at the nearness of her mouth. Without hesitation, she wrapped her fingers around it, giving a gentle tug. All the while smiling up at me with a smug little grin.

"Stop playing and open up, pretty girl. Let me feel your mouth."

"What if I want to make *you* beg for it?"

"You won't, because you love this as much as I do." I reached down and covered her hand with mine, squeezing hard. "You think I didn't notice you get yourself off last night while you sucked my cock? Number eight."

She froze, blinking twice. "You counted my orgasms?"

"When I bring a woman like you to her knees—literally and figuratively—you bet your perfect little ass I'm keeping track. I've got every single one locked away, including number ten I just gave you on the desk. Now it's my turn."

I tapped the head of my cock against her bottom lip, demanding entrance. My legs shook in anticipation, my balls already pulling tight from our back and forth. I loved how she gave as good as she got. How she challenged me at every turn. Combine that with the fact that I could still taste her on my tongue, could still see the way she'd opened up around my fingers, had completely given herself over to the pleasure…? I was nearly gone, and we'd barely gotten started. Remembering shit like that was going to make me come all over her face before she'd even taken a lick.

"Give me your tongue, baby." I brushed the head of my cock back and forth across her lips, painting them with the precome leaking from the tip. "Let me inside again."

She didn't lick me tentatively. Didn't take my balls in her mouth or swipe her tongue from base to tip and work me into a frenzy. No, she gripped the base of my cock, opened her mouth, and swallowed me whole.

"*Jesusfuck.*" I groaned, gripping the bun she had her hair gathered into. Tugging her closer to me. Needing her so much closer. "Christ, you're good at this. That's it…take me all the way."

She hummed around my length as she bobbed up and down, swirling her tongue around the head before sucking deep and doing it all over again. Hollowing her cheeks, she looked up at me, her unpainted lips spread tight around my cock, eyes heavy. Needy. Yeah, she liked this. She fucking *loved* it.

"Get your hands up here," I said through panting breaths. "No getting yourself off this time."

Her eyes flashed, but she did as I said, sliding her hands up my thighs and around my hips. Then she reached back to grip my ass, those sinful nails digging into my flesh, and pulled me deep, swallowing around my cock.

"Shit," I hissed, curling forward over her. I tightened my hold on her hair while brushing my other hand down her back until I could squeeze her perfect, upturned ass. Trying to think of anything but the feel of her warm, wet mouth around me, her nails digging into my ass cheeks. Anything but the fact that this commanding woman was on her knees for me. Forcing my focus to something else so I didn't come down her throat. I was so fucking close, but that wasn't how this was going to end. Not tonight. Not when I had no idea how many more chances I had with her.

"Enough." With a sharp smack to her ass, I pulled away. Stepped back from the ecstasy that was her mouth, all the while trying to catch my breath.

Kennedy was a vision as she leaned toward me, eyes heavy, lips swollen, and cheeks flushed. Her nipples were hard enough to cut glass, and I knew if I slipped my hand between her legs, I'd find her dripping wet.

Part of me wanted to throw her on the bed and bury my face in her pussy. Let my tongue explore her a little more. Have her come again and again and again on my mouth and then have her do it again on my cock. But not tonight. Not with the way I felt—mad at her for everything she and her family had brought to my front door. Mad at myself that I couldn't control myself enough around her to walk away.

"Are you ready to beg yet?" I asked, forcing a false calm into my voice.

"Nope."

Such a defiant little thing. I hated how much I loved it.

A slow smile spread across my mouth. I could play this game all night. With my eyes connected to hers, I stripped then plucked a condom from my wallet and tossed it on the bed next to her. "When you're ready to beg. In the meantime…" I stepped just out of her reach and gripped my cock. Gave a short tug. Swiped my thumb over the head, unable to contain the shudder that racked my body. "Look how hard you made me." A tight stroke from base to tip. "I'm leaking for you, baby. And you don't want it?"

With my other hand, I reached over, brushing my thumb across her lower lip. Her harsh breaths swept against my skin, reassuring me I wasn't in this alone. "Guess my fist will have to do tonight. Seems like such a waste, is all."

And then I stroked my cock in earnest, the same way I had that morning in the shower. The same way I'd be doing tomorrow night and every night for the foreseeable future, all to thoughts of her. To her flushed face, her perfect-tipped tits heaving with her panting breaths, the smooth sweetness of her pussy I could still taste on my tongue.

"AJ…" She reached for me, but I stepped back, not slowing my hand.

"Shit, pretty girl. You're going to make me come so hard, and I'm not even inside you." I sped up my hand, jerking my cock harder, tighter. "Should I come all over your pretty tits? Or maybe on those cocktease lips?"

"Please. I want your cock, AJ. I'll…beg for it."

Groaning, I squeezed the base of my cock hard enough to make my orgasm recede. A shiver zipped down my spine as I tried to calm my breathing. A fuck-lot of good it did me—not when Kennedy leaned toward me, trying to inch closer, her hands restless against her thighs. Needy. Desperate. "Knew you'd see it my way. Turn around. I wanna grip that ass while I fuck you."

"Such a dirty mouth. I'd tell you to fuck off if I didn't think you could live up to your filthy words." She spun around, presenting me with the gorgeously obscene view of her pert ass in the air, the glistening lips of her pussy peeking out from between her legs. Then she looked at me over her shoulder, her lip caught between her teeth. Eyes hooded and dark. Hair tousled thanks to my fingers, the bun no longer containing the wild strands.

"You ready for me?" I grabbed the condom and rolled it down my cock. Then I knelt behind her on the bed, gliding my hand over her upturned ass.

"Absolutely." She gave me a saucy little grin, complete with a goddamn wink. My feisty girl. "Fuck me, please."

I leaned over her, my lips right next to her ear as I

gathered her hair in my hand and wrapped it around my fist so I could tug her head back. "Knew you'd ask nicely before the end of the night."

And then I drove inside her in one deep thrust.

"Christ, baby," I said over her moans. "My memories didn't do this justice, did they? This morning, I tried to trick myself into thinking my fist was as good as your pussy." I leaned back, watching my cock disappear inside her as I gripped her ass with one hand and pressed my fingers in tight. Digging into her flesh, loving the thought of leaving another set of marks on her. "Nothing is, though. Isn't that right, pretty girl? I'm a slave to this pussy, and it's only been a day."

"Fuck, AJ. Please. *Please*." She clenched the sheets between her fists and bucked back against me, meeting my drives thrust for thrust, her keening cries near constant. Jesus, I'd done that—reduced this woman to a string of unintelligible curses and panting breaths.

"You're so worked up, all it's gonna take is a brush of my finger across your clit, and you're gonna be coming all over me, aren't you?" I leaned forward again, covering her back with my chest. Slipped my other hand around her hip and down toward her soaked pussy. Split my fingers in a V to avoid her clit. "Jesus, you love this, don't you? Love me telling you what to do, making you beg for it. You're fucking dripping."

"Yes. *Yes*. I'll beg more. Just don't stop."

"No more begging, baby. Let me feel it. Let me feel you squeeze my cock again." I finally gave us what we both wanted and brushed my fingers over her swollen clit at the same time I sank my teeth into the juncture of her neck and shoulder.

Kennedy reached back and gripped my thigh as she came with a scream, her back arched, legs opening even farther to take me deeper.

Groaning, I pumped through her release, thrusting into her harder and faster, desperate to lose myself in her. "Fuck, you feel so goddamn good. You're gonna make me come, pretty girl."

She rocked back into me, fucking herself against my cock. "You make me so wet. Feel it, handsome? That's all from you. Every drop."

That was it. I was a goner. Lips pressed to her neck, I sank as deep as I could, shuddering as my orgasm rocketed through me. Gripped her hip through it all. Kept her tight to me while I shuddered and emptied inside her.

All the while trying to forget what waited at the end of the evening. Trying to forget that we had no business being together, that I shouldn't even have been there. That the one girl I could see in my future was the one I could never have.

# chapter six

KENNEDY

THREE DAYS. It'd been three days since AJ had come to my room and made me beg for him, and they'd been the best days of my life. I'd expected AJ to leave right after he'd fucked me hoarse, but no. The man had stayed until the early hours of the morning. Had fucked me again and again, waking me up with his face between my legs or his hands tweaking my breasts. Had simply rolled over and started on another round whenever I'd reached for his cock. It'd been a night full of rough sex and harsh words, but I'd loved it.

Apparently, so had he, because we hadn't been able to stop. Lunch break during the workday? AJ snuck to the hotel to grab a quickie in my room. Charles on a conference call that I didn't need to participate in? I'd hurry over to Pops' Hops and drop to my knees for

AJ in his office. Every day and every night, we spent time together. And during all this, his anger faded. The sweetness and charm of the man I'd met that first night returned. I was falling for him, which only made things between us that much more bittersweet. Because as soon as Rochester Entertainment's real estate deal went through and we moved forward on building our brewery on Temperance Falls? He'd walk. I knew it. He knew it.

And there was nothing we could do about it.

I tried, though. No matter how adamant Charles was, I pushed him to halt this project. To change the restaurant concept. If he was a dog with a bone about closing other businesses, I was the same about not closing AJ's. I'd tried everything—taking Charles to the local four-star Italian place and dangling shutting that down with one of our high-end concepts, walking him down Main Street to show him how our quick-service cafes would fit the format of the tourist part of town. Hell, I even flat out told him the brewery would fail and provided him data to back up that claim. He didn't care. He wanted that gargantuan building completed ASAP—no ifs, ands, or buts.

I was running out of options.

So I reviewed contracts, forecasts, and market studies of the surrounding areas to try to find something my brother would accept as a reason not to open the brewery, and I spent whatever time I had with AJ. Unfortunately, Charles kept eating up more and more of that time, taking me away from what I truly wanted to be doing. Which wasn't spending my lunch hour with Charles.

"Why are we headed into town for lunch? I figured we'd stay at the hotel." I hurried to keep up with my brother's long stride, pissed I hadn't changed to a more sensible pair of shoes. I had assumed I'd meet up with AJ over lunch again, so I'd worn the highest, sexiest heels I'd brought with me. Not exactly run-after-your-asshole-brother appropriate.

"I wanted something different. Besides, there's a coffee place here that intrigues me. I wonder what sort of business model we'd need to adopt to get into that field."

I held back my groan. Coffee was a brutal industry, with major players already well established. There was no way we'd make the sort of money we'd need to in that space. Still, if Charles was thinking about coffee concepts, maybe he'd develop a new obsession and forget about beer.

Long shot, but it could happen.

"I can run analysis on the industry for that."

Charles waved me off as we reached the coffee shop. Bundt and Grind Café. Cute name.

"We'll deal with that after the brewery. I think this island is ripe for a few Rochester projects, but let's start with the one and see how the tourists respond.

Of course. The brewery. Jesus, the man had a one-track mind.

Inside, the coffeehouse fit the mold: low, comfy chairs, books, dark wood, pastry case, and soft, subtle music playing in the background. But all that faded as I spotted the man sitting at a table in the back. A man whom, even with his back to me, I'd know anywhere.

"Kennedy."

I jerked, my eyes wide as I met the frustrated stare of my brother. "What? Oh, medium latte."

The girl behind the counter nodded and headed to the espresso machine as I went back to studying AJ. He seemed to be reading a newspaper, his head bowed and one leg crossed over the other. The picture of casual. I wanted to strut over to him, rip the paper out of his hands, and straddle him right there in that seat. He'd left this morning after fucking me hard against the shower tiles, but I still wanted more. Still craved him. I even wore the death-trap heels for him, to entice him to wrap my legs around his waist and fuck me like the naughty girl I was with him.

Alas…Charles.

"I'll grab a table while you wait for your drink." He walked off, eyes down. Phone in hand. "And bring me a napkin, will you?"

Someday, I'd explode from all the sighs I was forced to hold in.

Seconds later, I grabbed my latte and followed Charles to a table. Of course, he picked the one right behind AJ. I held my breath as he pulled out a chair and took a seat, his eyes still locked on his phone. He hadn't even noticed AJ in the other chair, it appeared. Good—I didn't want to see the two get into a verbal sparring match. And as much as I wanted to spend time with AJ, I preferred to do it when my brother wasn't five feet away from me.

"Anthony says one of the suppliers is warning us about some sort of pig sickness." He scoffed, scrolling through the messages on his iPhone. "Why does our brother bother me with this shit?"

"It's his job as procurement and logistics manager. If there's a pig issue, then there's a pork shortage. And if there's a pork shortage, our cost of food goes up, affecting our ability to maintain inventory on the meats." I took a sip of my coffee, sneaking a peek over Charles' shoulder. AJ had noticed me—there was no doubt. His shoulders sat stiffer than before, his head turned to the side so I could see his profile. Jesus, the man was handsome. Fit and tanned and just plain gorgeous. And mine. At least, for a little while.

"Yes, well…we have staff to take care of those things."

"That staff would be Anthony and me—your siblings—and the teams below us. We still have to let you know what's going on in case you need to make a decision, dear CEO." I set my coffee down and sat back, seeing an opportunity to make sure AJ knew exactly what he was dealing with. "Charles, you pay me to make sure we have the best financial plans in place, to mitigate risks, and to provide business advice on what decisions would be the most profitable."

Charles huffed. "I swear to God, Kennedy. If you try to tell me again that a brewery here is a bad fit, my head will explode."

A girl could dream. "That's exactly what I'm going to tell you, and what I'll keep telling you. We could make three times the profit in half the time with a different restaurant concept. We could come in and open three casual spots on the main tourist strip for the cost of that one building across town. The math doesn't make sense."

"I don't care about math." Charles leaned forward, practically glaring at me. "I follow my gut, and my gut says we should build a brewery. You found me a good piece of property at a price in our budget. We're building a motherfucking brewery, and I'm tired of listening to you try to talk me out of it. Now, if you can't get on board with my plans, maybe we need to look for a different CFO who—"

His phone rang before he could finish his threat.

"I need to take this." Charles was up and out the door within seconds, leaving me fuming in my seat.

How dare that little shit threaten me. If it weren't for my help, he'd have run Rochester Entertainment into the ground years ago. I'd been handling the finances of the company before I even had my master's degree; I knew them better than anyone. Unlike Charles, my spot in the company had been earned with hard work, education, and skill…not simply having a penis and being lucky enough to be born first. My father had handed off the business to his three children with Charles as CEO, me as CFO, and Anthony CLO…equals in his mind. And now Charles was going to throw me out like a stray dog? As if we weren't running a family business together?

Fuck him.

"I know he's your brother and all, but man, that guy's a dick." AJ turned just a little in his seat, enough to shoot me a quick glance and a frown.

I sighed, chancing a look outside to make sure Charles couldn't see AJ and me chatting. "Yeah, well, my mother didn't breastfeed him long enough. It's the only reason I can think of for him to be such a big baby at times. My younger brother isn't anywhere near as needy."

AJ's warm chuckle made me grin, but it was the concern in his eyes as they swept over me that warmed my heart. And the rest of my body.

"You okay?"

"Other than the fact that my shoes hurt my feet and my job is in jeopardy, sure."

He bent down, taking a long look at my legs and feet. Licking his lips when he sat back up. Thank God for that elliptical machine at home.

"I like the shoes."

And just like that, the man had me in the palm of his hand. He practically fucking owned me. "I wore them for you."

He stared for a bit, cocking his head slightly. "You did, huh? And why's that?"

"I'd been hoping to come to Pops' for a little lunch-hour naughtiness against the wall. There's nothing better for a girl's confidence than for her lover to pick her up as if she weighs nothing, and you've got those gorgeous muscles just waiting to be put through a workout." I bit my lip, swinging my crossed leg enough to gain his attention. "But, alas. Duty called."

There was nothing better than seeing those green eyes of his darken, watching as he went from casual attraction to lust-filled devil in seconds. I loved that look. Craved it, really.

And he knew that. "'Duty' seems to be busy outside."

I turned to check, watching as my brother paced with his phone held to his ear. "Yes, it looks that way."

"You know what I love about Bundt and Grind?" AJ leaned closer, stealing all of my attention once more. "The single-stall bathroom with four perfectly acceptable walls."

It took me all of point-two seconds to make up my mind.

"Meet me there in two minutes." I stood slowly, straightening my skirt before walking to the waste can to throw away my paper cup. And yes, I made sure to sway my hips more than usual. Who could blame me? I took one last look outside as I strolled across the floor. If the way Charles gestured with his arms was any indication, the call wasn't going his way, which meant he'd argue and argue until he made sure to exhaust every single opportunity to turn that around. Perfect.

With a wink at AJ, I headed to the gender-neutral

bathroom in the back corner of the restaurant. The space was…nicer than I'd expected. Clean and bright with the toilet in a small water closet and a big, stone counter with a sink taking up one end beneath a huge mirror. This could be fun.

AJ joined me about fifteen seconds after I'd walked in, looking hot and bothered and so very fuckable as he locked the door behind him. But it wasn't in me to make things so easy on him.

"What happened to two minutes?"

"You think I can sit out there for two minutes, knowing you're in here waiting for me to fuck you?

"You're so impatient." I leaned up to give him a small kiss before backing away. He watched me, eyes dark, chest heaving. Cock hard. Oh yes, this would be fun.

When my back hit the stone counter, I hiked my skirt up to my waist and hooked my thumbs in the top my panties. I swear, if AJ's eyes got any darker, they'd be black, a fact that only ramped up my own arousal for him. Slowly, keeping my eyes on AJ's, I bent at the waist and pulled the silk and lace down and off, setting them in my purse before standing back up. Shaking, needful in all the right ways, I hopped up on the counter.

And then I spread my legs, letting him see exactly how wet and swollen I was for him already. "Ready when you are, handsome."

He didn't disappoint.

AJ was on me in a breath, inside me in mere

seconds. How he managed to get the condom on, I had no idea, but one moment he was kissing me desperately, and the next he had my ass pulled to the edge of the counter and was sliding inside me. He wasn't sweet or gentle either. Wasn't controlled in any way. Instead, he fucked me like he needed to, like he couldn't waste another second not being inside me. And that need? That desperation… It had me clenching around him in record time.

"Doesn't matter that I just fucked you early this morning, does it?" His fingers dug into my ass, pulling me closer, forcing my shoulders back and opening me wider for him. "I'll never get tired of being inside you."

"Fuck, AJ." I gripped his shoulders, my legs around his hips, one shoe having fallen off. His pelvis rocked against my clit, causing stars to form behind my eyes. Causing me to come with a gasp and a shake that rocked me from head to toe. AJ grunted and slammed home a few more times, pushing me back as he groaned through his own release. Rocking slowly into me as we came down. Kissing me sweetly as we both caught our breath.

I could do this every fucking day.

"I didn't even get to enjoy the shoes," he whispered against my ear, making me laugh.

"And I didn't get my wall sex, but this was a fine substitute." I licked across his bottom lip, nibbling softly just to hear him groan. "If it makes you happy, I'll wear the shoes tonight. I'll even put them on your shoulders while you lick my pussy."

He pulled back, dropping another soft kiss to my lips. "Now you're just taunting me."

Oh. He hadn't seen taunting yet. "I might even beg for it…if you make me."

Another groan, another deep kiss, and then AJ pulled away to deal with the condom.

"Do you have to go to work?" I cleaned up and pulled my skirt down, leaving the panties off. I could deal with those when I got back to the hotel. They were too wet to be comfortable.

"Yeah. Luke's meeting me there in twenty to…" He paused, his eyes darting away. Unable to look at me as he said, "go over things."

And just like that, the guilt flooded me. The anger. But I had to push it back, had to control it. I had so little time with AJ, and I needed not to dwell on the inevitable so I could take advantage of every single moment.

Like this one. AJ knelt before me, holding on to my leg gently as he slid my lost shoe back onto my foot. Looking like some sort of debauched Prince Charming. And when he glanced up, when he smiled at me from down on his knees, I was a goner.

Fuck, I was falling in love with him.

Maybe I already had. A thought which made me grab him by the chin and pull him to his feet. Made me wrap my arms around his neck and kiss him deeply, slowly, putting every emotion I felt for him into that kiss. Love, frustration, fear, need… everything. And he returned it with just as much.

Met me stroke for stroke as he held me tighter than anyone ever had before.

"I should go," I whispered, feeling slightly off-balance after breaking such a strong kiss. Slightly panicked at the idea of losing what we had.

"Me too." He kissed me again before slapping my ass. "Have a good day, pretty girl."

I headed for the door, my legs weak, my pussy wet and throbbing, and completely wrecked over the man. "You too, handsome. I'll see you later."

And then I was gone, leaving a piece of my heart with him.

Knowing I'd never get it back.

# chapter seven

AJ

WHEN I'D WALKED into Bundt and Grind for some coffee and one of their incomparable glazed croissants, I certainly hadn't set out for a little afternoon delight with the one woman who drove me out of my goddamn mind. But I'd never been one to turn up my nose at an opportunity. All it took from Kennedy was one twitch of her too-high, strappy shoes and the grin I'd come to know meant pure trouble, and I was reduced to incoherence.

The woman undid me.

And yet…we had no future. In a matter of days, she'd move forward on the project with her fuckstick of a brother, and that'd be it. I couldn't be in a relationship with someone who crushed my livelihood—and who took everything from my best friend while she was at it.

Shit…a relationship. I hadn't thought the word since…well, ever. I wasn't a relationship guy—never had been. When I'd been playing baseball, it'd just made sense. Sure, there were plenty of guys on the team with wives or girlfriends, but when you had cleat chasers throwing themselves at you after every game—and every waking second in between—it was better not to be tied down. Plus, to be perfectly fucking honest, commitment scared the living shit out of me.

But Kennedy made me wonder if maybe it wouldn't be too bad. Maybe waking up to her gorgeous face every morning, going to sleep with her body pressed up against mine, having her smile greet me when I got home was something I could live with.

Except that wasn't true either… She'd made me *crave* it. And wasn't that just a bitch.

I walked in the back door of Pops' Hops, not ready to deal with the customers yet, and headed straight for the office. The door was open, Luke bent over the desk, flipping through some papers.

He glanced up when I shut the door behind me, lifting his chin in greeting. "Hey, man." And then he said the same thing he had every day since this whole thing had started. "Anything new?"

I shook my head and sank into the leather couch. "Nothing good."

He sighed and dropped the papers on the desk. "Give me the not-good, then."

"Charles and Kennedy were at Bundt and

Grind. Sat right behind me, so I overheard their conversation."

"Yeah, and?"

"The fucker is like a dog with a chew toy. Kennedy told him point-blank it was a stupid move to open one of their breweries here. That it'd cost them a shitload of money, that the numbers don't add up, but the asshole doesn't care. It's like he's got a hard-on for ruining other businesses, no matter if it's at the expense of his own."

"Fuck. This doesn't look good, man." Stress and frustration bled into his voice, and I hated that I couldn't do anything to stop it. "You can't talk to her? See if she can get him to back off?"

If only he knew how well that'd worked last time. While I hadn't come right out and told him the details of my involvement with Kennedy, Luke wasn't an idiot. He'd known me long enough to figure out what was up between her and me a while ago. And, like the perfect best friend he was, he didn't mention the fact that maybe fucking our competition wasn't in our best interests.

I blew out a breath and rested my head against the back of the couch. "I've tried. Multiple times. I thought she was blowing smoke up my ass at first. But after hearing them today?" I shook my head and met Luke's stare. "She's doing everything she can. He's just not listening."

"We need to find out a way to *make* him listen. This isn't just a job, or even just a business. Everything

I've got is tied up in Pops'…my entire life savings. We can't lose this, AJ."

"I know."

We sat in silence, my mind spinning a mile a minute as I tried to come up with a magical solution I hadn't already thought of and exhausted. The only way I could see out of this was by relying on other people to be decent human beings. Two run-ins with the shitstain that was Charles Rochester were enough to know he didn't have an ounce of decent in his body.

"It serious?" Luke's voice broke through the quiet, his eyes steady on me.

"What?"

"Whatever you're doing with Kennedy."

"What? No. No, it's just…" I swallowed, the words feeling bitter against the back of my throat. "It's just sex."

The words were exactly as convincing as they felt. Luke's stare said he didn't buy it, but he was too good of a friend to call me out on it.

———

It was late by the time I slipped into Kennedy's hotel room with the key she'd given me a couple nights before. My schedule at the brewery wasn't exactly conventional, which meant late-night calls or none at all. Kennedy had chosen the late-night—or, more accurately, very early morning—wake-ups.

I'd spent most of my evening at Pops' trying to convince myself that the words I'd spoken to Luke had been true. That this thing between Kennedy and me started and ended with sex, pure and simple.

Except there was this niggling voice in my head, this ache in my chest whenever I tried to pretend, that told me otherwise. The problem was, it *couldn't* be anything more. Which meant I needed to convince myself real damn quick that this was just a fling. That Kennedy and I could never be more than just two ridiculously compatible people who had off-the-charts sex.

Motion-activated lights along the floor lit up as I stripped on the way to the bed, tossing my clothes as I went. Kennedy was a sight—completely naked and sprawled out, arms and legs every which way, the sheets twisted around one ankle. I tried not to think about how a wild sleeper like her could tuck herself against me when I shared her bed. Tried to ignore the memory of her curled up into my side, her head on my chest. How perfectly we'd fit together.

Shaking the thoughts from my head, I climbed onto the bed, running my hand along her leg as I settled between her spread thighs. I'd woken her up like this enough times to predict what her reaction would be.

I ran my nose up her inner thigh, licking a path where her leg met her body. And then I couldn't wait. Not when her pussy was so close, the tiny strip of hair at the top practically a beacon for my tongue. Even a single second more without her taste would be too long.

Spreading her open with my thumbs, I licked a long, slow line up the length of her slit, smiling against her pussy when she sighed in her sleep. Her hips started rolling, just as they always did, her dreams still keeping her under. But I needed her awake for this. Needed to hear her moans, her breathy sighs of my name. Needed to feel her hands in my hair trying to get me to do what she wanted.

So I held her open, fastened my lips around her clit, and sucked. And no sound in the world could beat the surprised gasp she gave when she first came to.

"AJ?"

I hummed against her pussy, pulling back to flick my tongue against her clit. "Were you expecting someone else?"

The thought sent a wave of jealousy through me, but I pushed it aside. There was no room for jealousy in what we had.

"No, I just…don't stop." She reached down, threaded her fingers through my hair, and tugged me to her.

I gave her thigh a sharp nip, hard enough to let her know I didn't take kindly to her telling me what to do when I had my mouth on her pussy, but I didn't stop. I let her have her way, because I wanted it just as badly as she did, wanted to feel her come undone from just my touch.

Cupping her ass, I lifted her to me and fit my mouth over her pussy, swiping my tongue through her slit. Exploiting all her weaknesses I'd found over the past week. The places that made her gasp and moan, made her sigh with pleasure, made her ride my face even as I held her suspended off the bed.

"Jesus, I love your mouth. You're going to make me come so hard."

I groaned against her as she did exactly as she promised. Fingers locked in my hair, she moaned through her release, the sounds loud enough for me to hear even through her legs clenched tight around my head. I kneaded her ass as I settled her back against the bed. Brought her down from her high with soft swipes of my tongue against her oversensitized flesh, brushing the stubble below my lower lip over her clit every few passes.

She shuddered, her body quaking in the aftershocks. "More, AJ. I want more of you."

With one last lick of her pussy, I pulled away and reached for the condoms we'd taken to storing in the drawer of the bedside table and slipped one on as I looked down at her. She'd left the curtains parted, and the moonlight off the lake lit up the space enough so it made her skin glow.

"Jesus, you're gorgeous," I said before I could stop myself.

She opened her mouth to respond, but I cut off her reply with my mouth, slipping my tongue against hers. Locking her legs around my hips, she rocked up against me, falling into a rhythm when the head of my cock nudged her clit with each pass.

"You too tired to do some work, baby?"

"Not if it gets us both off."

I smiled against her lips, then rolled us until she sat astride my hips. Of all the positions we'd tried over the past week—and we'd tried a metric fuck-ton—this was my favorite. I loved watching her face as she lined me up, then took me inside, making us both groan. Loved the feel of her hips under my hands, their fullness begging for my fingers to leave their mark.

Hands braced on either side of my head, she leaned over me, her hair surrounding us like a dark curtain. She rolled her hips in a soft, subtle pattern, just enough to drive me crazy with want. Enough to make me want to grip those lush hips, hold her in place above me, and pound into her from below.

From the look she shot me, she knew it too. Was counting on it.

Too bad I wasn't ready for the finish yet.

I wanted this torture, wanted every minute of it. Wanted to remember in vivid detail how she arched her back against me when I sucked one of those perfect tits into my mouth. How she tightened her legs against my sides the closer she got to her release. How, when she wanted just a little more, she pressed her hands on my chest and sat upright, taking me as deep as she could, shuddering as she rolled her hips in a torturous circle.

Christ, I could watch her do this every night for the rest of my life and never get sick of it. Never go looking for anything else. Never worry about the confines of commitment. Because she was a woman I could commit myself to without hesitation.

The thought made me close my eyes, as if I could block it out. Block out the knowledge of what being with her felt like. The knowledge of what I'd be missing once she was gone.

She dropped down again, her hips rolling faster, harder. Thumbs stroking my jaw, she nipped my lower lip. "Open your eyes, AJ. I want you to see what you do to me."

Unable to deny her, I dragged my eyes open and looked into hers. They were half-lidded and glazed, a sure sign she was on the precipice, ready to fall over. I tried not to think of anything else as I gripped her neck and pulled her down for a kiss, slipping my other hand to the small of her back and encouraging the slow roll of her hips.

It didn't take long for her to drive us both exactly where we needed to go. I licked my way into her mouth and swallowed her moans as she came around me, my orgasm chasing hers.

Kennedy finally broke away from the kiss, her breaths harsh against my neck as I struggled to catch my own. Not from the weight of her boneless form collapsed against my chest, but from the fact that the whispered words in my head the past week had been right.

I'd lied to Luke and myself when I'd said this was only sex. That my time with her was nothing more than a fling.

She was the real fucking deal. And I had to let her go.

# chapter eight

KENNEDY

THE PROBLEM WITH early morning meetings was that it took me a couple of hours to erase the time spent with AJ the night before from my thoughts. Usually, those thoughts were like fond memories—moments spent together where his hand had hit just the right spot or his voice had broken while I'd had his cock in my mouth. Good memories—the kind that wound me up to see the man later in the day.

I would have given anything to be fighting off those types of thoughts. Instead, my mind refused to focus because AJ had been different last night. Distant. Something in his eyes, in the way he left me with barely a kiss, had sent ice shooting down my spine and made me slightly unbalanced all morning. There was no doubt in my mind why. The signs of him pulling away were evident, and there was nothing

I could do to stop him. I didn't even know if he realized what he was doing—how he was putting distance between us—but I did. I saw it. And I hated it.

"You need to send the purchase agreement today." Charles tossed the paperwork he'd been looking over across the table. We'd been reviewing listings, zoning guidelines, and project scopes for over an hour already. All things we'd gone over a hundred times, all the steps that would lead us to buying the property for the brewhouse.

And end my relationship with AJ.

"We could bid on the last outlet spot at the mall project instead." I pulled out the folder for that property. "The infrastructure is already in place, which would make the overall project less costly. Plus, the location is ideal. Great street, good traffic counts, the mall renovation will lend residents and businesses—"

"It's not big enough. We can't fit the full brewery experience footprint there, so it's out, and the ones that are sized right are priced out of our budget. I want the Marina Street lot. It's the only piece available without zoning restrictions, and it's in our price range."

"Barely. It's barely in our price range. If someone else makes an offer even just a few thousand over ours—"

"Kennedy."

I looked up, frowning at Charles' glare. "What?"

"Stop being a roadblock and get on board

with this plan, or I'll send you home and bring in Anthony to assist me."

My shoulders pulled tight, my back stiffening as a fire of pure rage built within me. "Excuse me?"

"You heard me." He stood, pacing the length of his hotel room. "I'm tired of fighting over this, I'm tired of you telling me how I'm going to fail…I'm exhausted by your negativity."

"Giving you the data that says you won't make money on a deal isn't negativity. It's reality."

"But it's one I don't choose to accept, and I've been clear about that. My breweries will be built how I want them, and they will make money. You're just too shortsighted to see it."

There was something about listening to a man who had less education than I did—who didn't understand the same concepts and strategies I'd spent years developing—try to dismiss my job. It made me want to knock his head right off his stubby neck. "No, Charles. I'm not shortsighted—you're forgetful. Do you not remember how much money we lost because you were convinced a pirate-themed restaurant was a good idea?"

He crossed his arms, looking mulish. And defensive. "That concept not working was because of the recession."

"Or because it was a shit idea." I sat back as he fumed, finally ready to pin him down on a few things. If he was going to throw my job in my face, I'd throw a few things in his. "How about how you just *knew* our highest-earning Italian chain should become a seafood-only restaurant? We lost what…almost twelve million dollars in gross sales plus expenditures on revamping the entire chain twice that year? The high-end sandwich shop? Failed. The small plates restaurants you thought would be a great fit in the Midwest? Failed. And on each decision you made, I warned you against it because my forecasts said they wouldn't work. Your track record is far worse than mine, big brother. Perhaps you're the one who should be worried about keeping their job."

"Get out." He stormed across the room and threw open the door. "Get the fuck out of this room and don't talk to me again today unless it's to tell me you've sent a purchase agreement that fits within our budget on the property I want. Once you do, go home. I don't need you here. Anthony and I will discuss your insubordination and attitude when I get back to New York."

"You're making a mistake again, Charles. The board will have your ass if you keep losing money on these harebrained ideas."

"Get out," he yelled, his face bright red.

I sighed and collected my papers, shaking my head. "I'll send your fucking purchase agreement, but then I'm going to the board. Your ego is driving the ship, and Rochester Entertainment can no longer afford to support that."

"Purchase agreement. Today."

As if I were a dog waiting to answer his commands.

"You'll get your land, even if I think it's the stupidest thing you've ever done."

I stalked past him, cradling the messy paperwork in my arms. Charles slammed the door behind me, making the frame shake. Such a temper, which seemed to be a family trait if my own fury was any indication. Anthony was the only calm one in the family. Maybe he should be assigned to travel with Charles, after all.

When I reached my room, I stormed inside and tossed the folders and papers on my bed, unable to stop thinking about Charles and his threats. That fucking bastard. Who did he think he was? This was a family business, not just his. And though I doubted Anthony or the board would agree to firing me, I doubted Charles and I would recover from this fight. One, because of his temper. Two, because he refused to listen to me on financial matters. And three, no matter how much I hated admitting it, because of his disdain for AJ. If Charles were a halfway decent human being, he wouldn't be looking forward to shutting down small businesses. But he not only looked forward to it, he actively made choices that would be detrimental to others... and that fact wasn't likely to change. It also wasn't what I wanted to be part of.

Frustrated, too antsy to work, I paced. Wishing I could call AJ. Wanting him with me so I could rant and rave over Charles, and he could...I don't know. Listen? Offer advice? Fuck, I'd never needed a man to help me with a problem, and I still didn't. But as I paced, my fingers itched to grab my phone. To call. To text. It wasn't need, though…it was want. I *wanted* his comfort, his calmness, his sense of humor. I wanted him to listen to me and offer support with his presence. To give me a hug and a slap to my ass that reminded me he was there for me. That he cared.

I wanted him, and as soon as I sent the purchase agreement I'd been holding on to over to the listing real estate agent, I was going to lose him.

When I was finally calm enough to deal with the shit left on my plate, I sat down at my table and pulled up the paperwork. I wanted to review it one more time before sending it, wanted to make sure I knew every word and detail before I did Charles' dirty work. Before I put the final nail in AJ's and my coffin.

But as I looked over numbers and figures, something that was so simple and clear struck me. Something I should have noticed before, had I stopped looking at the project as a whole and focused on the smallest details.

How could I have been so blind? Needing confirmation, I jumped up and rushed to the bed, digging through the paperwork until I found the two sheets I needed—the total budget for the project and the local market projections for each of Rochester Entertainment's different restaurant types. The plot of land was expensive—right at the top of our budget. Our offer left no real room for negotiation, but that was because Charles assumed the owner wouldn't get another one. The lot had been empty a long time, and the mall project had attracted any large-scale retail and restaurant attention. Charles was betting on the owners being happy to have an offer at all.

But what if he was wrong?

I grabbed my laptop, settled in on my bed so I could have all the paperwork before me, and started drawing up projections, options, cost analysis information, and reviewing concept proposals from the past few years. And when I had it figured out, when I had the final pieces of the puzzle in place, I sent the purchase agreement for Charles.

And then I grabbed my purse and hurried out the door. I needed to find AJ.

# chapter nine

AJ

ONE OF THE benefits of living on the island my entire life was not a whole lot happened around here without my knowing about it. Whether it was Margie cheating on that poor bastard Bob, or Frank's Deli being close to bankruptcy…or the fact that the lot on Marina Street had received a significant offer today—not their asking price, but damn close to it. That lot had sat empty for years, and now, coincidentally, had an offer on it the same week the Rochesters had arrived on Temperance Falls.

It didn't take a genius to put two and two together and figure out who'd put in that bid.

And I was certainly no genius. That much was confirmed when I realized the woman I'd somehow managed to fall for—despite doing everything in my power to try to avoid it—had purchased land in my hometown with the sole intent to put my partner and me out of business.

Fuck, that hurt.

After tearing my labrum during my first season in the majors, I'd thought it'd been painful hearing the surgeons say I had a better chance of winning the lottery than I did of pitching in the major leagues again. Getting a once-in-a-lifetime chance to play baseball for a living and having it snatched away had devastated me. But the truth was, that had nothing on this. Had nothing on losing Kennedy. I loved baseball with everything in me—had always loved it. But it didn't compare to her…didn't compare to the woman who'd managed to turn me inside out in only a week. Shit, had it really only been a week?

I blew out a breath, scrubbing the bar top at Pops' harder than necessary. I could do fuck all about it now. She'd made her choice, and it was time for me to get my head out of my ass and get shit done. Even though it felt like she'd ripped my heart from my chest, I still needed to get my head in the game and figure out what Luke and I needed to do to grow Pops' Hops' revenue by leaps and bounds before that cookie-cutter chain was up and running.

I didn't know anything about Charles other than the fact that he was a first-class dickhead, but I'd bet my left nut he rushed through projects. Didn't care how they got done, just that they did so as quickly as possible, and he had the money to make it so. I gave us mere months to figure this shit out. That meant I didn't have time for silly things like heartbreak.

In the time since I'd come to Luke with the news of the offer, we hadn't said much. Instead, we'd stewed silently—me, scrubbing an already shining bar top while he vigorously dried the mugs. Last time he'd been this worked up, Hannah had been on the line. Now it was a little thing like his livelihood and entire life savings. No big deal.

"You know," I said, trying for the tenth time to offer what I had more than enough of, "I'm happy to—"

"Goddammit, AJ, stop with the fucking offers," he said between clenched teeth. "I want to exhaust every other option before we even *think* about having to dip into your savings to cover the overhead here."

I clenched my teeth and blew out a deep breath, scrubbing harder at a nonexistent spot. Stubborn bastard would never accept anything from me above and beyond what he matched, even if I put it straight into the business. He wanted to be equal partners in every way. Didn't matter that I had piles of money I didn't know what to do with and couldn't possibly spend in my whole lifetime.

I'd been so young when I'd gotten my signing bonus that my parents had made damn sure I hadn't spent it recklessly…had made sure I'd invested and been smart about my earnings. And, really, what did a single, twentysomething guy need anyway? I had a house and a car, and I lived on a fucking island. So, the money sat.

Truth be told, I couldn't blame Luke for his stance. If the roles were reversed, I wasn't so sure I wouldn't do the same damn thing. Which meant I needed to figure out some other way for us to keep the business afloat even in the face of what was coming. There had to be an option I was overlooking because of my tunnel vision over the threat of Pops' Hops' security on the line.

I stopped scrubbing and tossed the rag under the counter. "I'm gonna head into the office. Crunch some numbers."

"The fucking numbers haven't changed, man." He slammed down the mug he'd finished drying on the bar top, the action drawing a few of the regulars' eyes.

I gave the customers my best "nothing to see here" smile and turned to Luke. "Hey, asshole, what did I tell you about those fucking mugs? What'd they ever do to you? Don't take your anger out on 'em, Rocky."

He slid me a look out of the corner of his eye as he picked up another glass and started drying it. "Better I take it out on an inanimate object, don't you think?"

I couldn't argue with him there. Much as I loved the idea of punching Kennedy's smug-ass brother right in his smug-ass mouth, it wouldn't serve either of us to get arrested for assault. "Look, I know the numbers haven't changed, but *something* has to. You do the brews, and I do the business… That was the plan from the start, right?"

A muscle ticked in his jaw as he continued to wipe the already dry glass. "Your point?"

"My point is, I need you to trust me on this. I'll *find* a way, Luke. Pops' isn't going anywhere."

I only hoped I wasn't spewing false promises.

Once in the office, I went straight for the laptop, searching the property listings on the island for the land Kennedy and her brother had put a bid in on. It was at the southern end of Marina Street, which meant no foot traffic but plenty of people heading for the beach and docks. And it was priced reasonably, probably because it'd been on the market so long. In fact, we'd looked at it when we'd first decided to start Pops' Hops.

While Luke and I had wanted an original building, something that had been on the island for decades, the plan had also been to house more tanks than we had room for here—really allow Luke the freedom to play with different recipes and try new brews. In the end, we'd nixed the possibility because we'd decided to start smaller. Test out the waters before investing in something of that magnitude. The plan had been to readdress it in a couple years. Find a lot close by the brewery to house an outbuilding filled with just tanks. Close enough that we could get to it easily without it being a hideous eyesore next to Pops' rustic building.

And while Pops' was doing well enough to pay us generous yearly salaries and put a good chunk into the business account every month, we had nowhere near what we'd need in order to expand right now.

*We* didn't. But I sure as hell did.

It took me all of five seconds of contemplation before I picked up the phone and dialed Brandon Catalpa, the agent who'd helped us secure Pops' Hops' building. Luke would be pissed as hell, but he'd get over it eventually.

If it meant saving both our livelihoods, his entire life savings, and his stepfather's legacy, well… I wasn't going to ask permission. I'd beg forgiveness when it was all said and done.

———

Several hours and many phone calls later, it was complete. Or as complete as it could be pre-negotiations. I was the proud soon-to-be owner of a huge-ass piece of land… and one soon-to-be pissed-off best friend. I went into the deal aggressively, and the sellers had accepted my generous offer with no hesitation. Amazing what a little money could do for you.

The door to the office opened, and without glancing up from the papers Brandon had faxed over, I breathed out a sigh. There was no way to ease the blow of this, but it'd be better to get it over with. Tell Luke now before he heard it elsewhere. "I'm glad you're here. I wanted to talk to you about—"

Except when I looked up, it wasn't Luke standing

in the doorway, but Kennedy. Christ, had it only been this morning that I'd learned she'd stomped all over my heart after playing with it inside my chest for a while? Taunting me with what I couldn't have before taking it all away for good.

She looked as composed as ever in her sleeveless, light green silky-looking shirt, black pencil skirt highlighting some of my most loved parts, and death traps—also known as my favorite fucking shoes—on her feet. Meanwhile, I was in faded jeans, a T-shirt, and a backward baseball cap, feeling about as put together as I looked.

How she could be standing in front of me after what she'd done and I still wanted to lose myself in her, I'd never know. And that only pissed me off more.

I tossed the papers on the desk and leaned back in the chair, pretending like the sight of her in those shoes that had been propped on my shoulders only a couple nights before didn't make my cock twitch. Pretending like seeing her in my space didn't make me ache with want. "Sorry, sweetheart, but the fuck factory is closed."

"I assume that means you heard Rochester Entertainment made an offer on a parcel of land."

I raised my eyebrows, surprised she wasn't denying it. Wasn't even trying to sugarcoat it. "That's what happens when you've lived here your whole life—you get told shit you might've been happier not knowing."

"I forget about small-town gossip mills sometimes. They're faster than Twitter."

"That's not the only thing you forgot about, apparently."

The hurt look she shot me pierced my chest—but, no. No fucking way was she going to make me feel bad for her. *She* was the one who'd decided to throw this away. It may only have been a week, but it'd felt like a hell of a lot longer than that to me. It'd felt *real*.

"Look," I said, "I don't have a lot of time for small talk, what with me trying to save our business and all. Is there a reason you're here?"

She cleared her throat and straightened her spine, pressing her shoulders back as she met my gaze straight on. "I have a business proposition for you."

I breathed out a laugh, shaking my head. She had some gall, showing up here after making a move to put us out of business and then propositioning me. It didn't matter that I'd stopped it—*she* didn't know that. "I already told your brother to fuck off. I thought that was pretty clear."

"I'm not here on behalf of my brother. In fact, I'll be leaving Rochester Entertainment in"—she lifted her wrist and glanced down at her watch—"about two hours. So I need you to put aside your anger for that long and listen to me. Please."

Her words caused the proverbial record scratch in my head. She had plans to leave her family's business? Why the hell would she do that? Why would she give all that up?

Hope, full and fierce, bloomed in my chest, but

I forced it down. Hope had gotten me a whole lot of fuck all the past week. "Does that mean you didn't put in the offer on behalf of your family's business?"

She hesitated for only a moment. "I did—there was no getting around Charles' desire to send that purchase agreement, but that was only after I spent all afternoon poring over information on the project. And while I couldn't stop him from sending his offer, I think I found a way around him."

Despite the fact that I'd already found my own way around her brother, I couldn't stop my curiosity over what she'd planned. "Found a way around him—how?"

"I'm going to buy the land he wants."

A punch to the face would've shocked me less than those words out of her mouth. "You're going to what?"

She sat at one of the chairs in front of the desk, crossing her legs before she pulled a folder out of her bag and slid it across the desk toward me. "Once I give my resignation letter to Rochester Entertainment, I'm sending my own purchase agreement to the listing agent. It'll beat out Charles' offer and be above his overall budget for property acquisition."

I couldn't believe what I was hearing…couldn't believe what she'd made plans to do. Flipping open the folder, I glanced at the papers within. Page after page of revenue forecasts and concept proposals and market research. She'd even included a sample menu.

I met her eyes. "You want to open a restaurant on Temperance Falls?"

She dipped her chin in acknowledgment. "My *own* restaurant. One I know can succeed without putting anyone local out of business."

*Her* restaurant—a way for her to get out from under her controlling, demeaning ass of a brother *and* stay here with me. A perfect fucking outcome.

And one that would never be because I'd bought the damn property right out from under both of them.

"Why would you do that?" I asked, desperate to know if she felt even half of what I did, or if I was alone in this thing. "Why would you go against your family for someone you've known a week?"

Her shoulders dropped, her mouth turning down at the corners. Disappointment cloaked her, but I wasn't sure why. "It's not just about you, AJ."

Of course not. That'd be crazy, and obviously, I was the only crazy one in the room. Even knowing this, hearing her say the words made that same disappointment I'd seen on her sit heavy on my shoulders. "No? What's it about then?"

"It's about me. Making a choice to be the type of businesswoman I want to be." She shook her head, breaking our gaze. "I've worked in restaurant operations my entire adult life. But as a child and a teenager, I worked in the restaurant my dad owned. That's how Rochester Entertainment began—one little steak house that had been my mother's dream. Half the herbs and vegetables they used came from her garden, and she taught me how to use them well. She loved that place, so after her death, my dad took their success and built more. I don't want more—I want simple. Good food acquired as locally as possible in a casual place at a decent cost for the non-tourist crowd."

She spoke more passionately than I'd ever heard her, even when she'd been discussing outlooks with Charles that day in Bundt and Grind. This was something she wanted with everything she had. Something she wanted *here*. And even though she'd just told me it wasn't because of me, something didn't add up. Not with the way she'd been with me, how we'd fit together. She could build her dream in a hundred different small towns, a dozen different domestic islands. And yet, she wanted to stay.

"Why Temperance Falls?"

She shrugged and looked down, suddenly finding the hem of her top very interesting. "I like the island, and the market is perfect for my idea."

Kennedy didn't get shy. She didn't do awkward or uncertain, which only proved my hunch right. She was exactly where I was, feeling everything I did.

I braced my elbows on the desk and leaned forward. "It seems you're not the only one who thinks the market is perfect."

She lifted her head, brow furrowed. "What do you mean?"

"A purchase agreement's already been accepted on the lot you were looking at."

Her mouth dropped open, eyes wide. And then she fumbled for her bag and pulled out her phone, fingers flying over the screen. A few seconds later, she shook her head. "But…I don't have an acceptance email. Who bid for it?"

"Does it matter?"

She sat still for a moment, and then emotions flicked over her face. Disappointment, frustration, sadness. Jesus, the sadness about crushed me. "I guess not." She smoothed a nonexistent wrinkle out of her shirt, pretending like everything was normal. Like I hadn't seen how much that news had crushed her spirit. "So long as it's not another brewery, you should be okay."

And that right there was why, despite every logical reason telling me to run away from her, I'd fallen anyway. She cared. She could pretend like she didn't, pretend like Temperance Falls was just an idyllic location for her dream restaurant, but the truth was, she cared. About *me*.

Balls to the wall time.

"I didn't take you as someone to get upset over a stalled business venture," I said. "You sure it wasn't more than that?"

Her nostrils flared with her deep inhale as she squared her shoulders and narrowed her eyes. "Don't expect me to say I'm staying for you, because I'm not. You're just…an added benefit."

I hummed, tilting my head to the side as if recalling some of those times. Like I had to do anything but blink to see her spread out in front of me, on top of me, beneath me. To remember her parted lips as she came, her smiling face in the light of the sunrise, her soft kisses to my neck when she thought I was already asleep.

"We had a lot of benefits, didn't we?" I pushed back from the desk and slipped around it, not stopping until I stood directly in front of her. Bracing my hands on the desktop on either side of me, I leaned back against it and crossed my ankles. "Did I tell you about our original idea for Pops' Hops? Initially, we'd wanted to have a space large enough to house dozens of tanks. So Luke could really experiment with different brews—try new recipes. We couldn't at the time because we didn't have equal capital for it." I shrugged. "But shit happens and things change. I couldn't very well sit by and let my best friend's dream die, could I?"

She stared at me, eyes wide, mouth agape. "You didn't."

"I did. It was my purchase agreement that was accepted." Accepted, but not binding. Not yet. "But I'd back out in a heartbeat if it meant you could open your dream restaurant." I reached out and ran my finger from her temple to her jaw. "If it meant you'd be able to stay with me."

She blinked up at me, lips parted. "You're serious?"

I pushed away from the desk and squatted in front of her, my hands gripping her hips. "That depends… Can you see yourself staying here for more than just the restaurant? Because if you say no, I was obviously joking the whole time, and we'll just pretend my heart isn't cracked open."

"AJ." Cupping my face, she leaned forward and brushed her lips against mine. "It's more than a restaurant that makes me want to stay."

"Yeah?" I couldn't hold back my smile even if I tried. Couldn't stop myself from kissing her either. Against her lips, I asked, "It's the Pilsner, isn't it?"

Her laughter blew against my mouth. "Totally. I dream of shandies now." She wrapped her arms around my neck, pulling me closer. "Shandies and you at the end of a long day sounds damn near dreamlike."

Jesus, the idea of Kennedy greeting me at the end of the day? Being the person I called when I had good news or bad? The one I wrapped myself around each night and woke up to each morning?

"Not dreamlike, pretty girl." I linked my fingers at the small of her back and tugged her to the edge of the seat. Needing her closer, even with her hands playing with the back of my hair, her lips millimeters from mine. "It sounds goddamn perfect."

# chapter ten



UNLESS YOU WANT me to climb under the table and plant my face between those legs, you're going to have to stop shaking them."

I slammed my feet to the floor and whipped around, meeting AJ's casual smile. The other diners in the hotel restaurant were too far away to hear him, thank goodness. They didn't need to be picturing his face between my thighs over their scrambled eggs and toast. Of course, with him sitting so close to me, I couldn't *not* picture it. The man was a master of distraction.

We'd celebrated our business coup all night in our own way, which meant hours upon hours of naked time. Something I was very much looking forward to getting back to, but we had one last job to do. The final thread to tie up before he could tie *me* up.

I really needed to get my mind off sex.

"Stop looking at me as if I'm something to eat," I whispered, leaning closer to him. "Your sexiness is making me nervous."

He covered my hand with his, squeezing tight. "You need to relax, pretty girl."

I nodded, shooting a glance at the door to the hotel restaurant again. The same door I'd been staring at since we sat down. "I know. I will. I just…want this over."

AJ nuzzled my neck, biting once before licking away the sting. "I bet I could make you loosen up…"

One-track mind. "Stop trying to make me think about sex while I'm ramping up to deal with my brother. The two streams should never cross."

His sigh sounded heavy, but he smiled as he moved to a respectable distance from me. "It was worth a shot." But AJ wasn't one to ignore me. He kept a hand on the back of my chair, kept a thumb rubbing along my nape. Kept in contact. "You're going to do great. And I'll be here as your muscle if you need me."

"Thanks. I might take you up on that if he insults Pops' Hops again. The man wouldn't know a well-run brewery if it smacked him in the face and started to wiggle."

Chuckling under his breath, AJ nodded to the waiter as he passed, making a motion to order another round of mimosas. Apparently, we were going to get drunk at breakfast. Something I would probably need once I was through with Charles.

As if that thought called to the devil himself, my brother came strutting into the dining room, a confident, professional businessman. I saw past his veneer, though. He was still pissed, and the anger flashing in his eyes only grew when he saw my table guest.

"Showtime," I whispered, pulling my hand from AJ's and grabbing my napkin. He sat back, casual as fuck, looking like sin incarnate sitting next to me. "Behave."

"Mmm…probably not."

I really hadn't expected him to.

"What was that email about last night?" Charles stormed the table, practically looming over me. "You can't quit on me."

I wiped my mouth with my napkin and sat back, regarding him as coolly as I possibly could. "I can, and I did. You were the one who said if I couldn't get on board with your plans, you'd call someone else out to do my job. Well, here's your chance. Replace me."

Charles shot a glare at AJ. "Kennedy, I think we need to head somewhere private to talk this out."

"No. There's nothing to talk about. I quit. Good luck, and maybe I'll see you at the family Christmas party."

AJ laughed, hiding it behind a cough. Not well, though. Charles turned on him, his alligator smile firmly in place.

"Mr. Phelps. Trying to sweet-talk my sister into coming to work for you? Maybe hoping you can gain access to some company secrets to save your sorry little brewery? That's bad form."

AJ glanced at me, giving me the opportunity to step in, but I simply nodded. He could handle this part. "Pops' doesn't need any of your shitty brewing 'secrets.' *You* tried to hire *us* because our brew was so good, remember?"

Charles' frown slid straight into a glower. "Beer is the easy part—the business side will eat you alive. Are you running in the black over there yet? Or are you still losing money?"

But AJ was far too cocky to be goaded. He rocked back in his chair and crossed his arms over his chest, still smiling. "You know what's great about this exchange? I can just…not answer your questions and not give a single fuck about doing so."

The color red Charles turned could only be described as tomato. "Let's go, Kennedy. I want to talk to you about the property deal for the brewery before I release you from service."

"Pretty sure my resignation was my release, jackass." I sat back, widening my eyes as if surprised. "Oh, but wait, did you not get my other emails? There is no property deal. Someone outbid us."

Charles jerked back as if I'd hit him. I sort of wished I had. The look on his face was pretty priceless.

"We researched for weeks. There was no other interested party. Who the fuck outbid us?"

AJ grinned in a way that screamed he was the cat who caught the canary. And I guess he was. "I did."

"With whose funding?" Charles stepped closer, pointing his finger in my face. "We're not backing this deal, Kennedy. Rochester Entertainment wants that property for a brewery, not for…whatever the fuck he's planning to do with it."

I shrugged. "I had nothing to do with the funding."

"Looks like you should've done a little more research on your competition, Chuck." AJ slid an arm around my shoulder, leaning over me. "It's probably hard for you to believe because I don't walk around with a permanent stick up my ass like you do, but I could buy that property many times over. In cash."

"This is bullshit," Charles spat, throwing his arms in the air.

But I'd dealt with enough of his tantrums over the past few years. I was done. "No, Charles. This is reality. The land is sold, so your brewery plan is over. And I already tendered my resignation, so my having to discuss business with you is also over. Now, if you'll excuse us, we're trying to have a nice breakfast before starting our day."

"So, what? You're going to give up everything to stay here on this nothing little island with no job to be with this *beer* man? I thought you were smarter than that."

"Oh, I have a job. Didn't I tell you? It must have slipped my mind, what with all the complaining you've been doing." I grabbed AJ's hand, weaving my fingers between his. "See, AJ here was kind enough to work with me on a build-to-lease deal. I figure it's time to go back to my roots—a nice, casual restaurant just like what Mom always loved running."

Charles sneered. He actually sneered at me. "You'll never make as much money as you did working for us with that plan. That's why Dad expanded—to be a success."

"Money isn't really my definition of success. Happiness is." I turned just enough to face AJ before planting a soft, sweet kiss on those horribly naughty lips of his. "And I'm really fucking happy right now."

My brother was silent for a long moment before finally huffing a breath. "Don't expect to come crawling back to the family business when you fail."

But Charles no longer mattered. AJ had captured my attention fully, his green eyes holding mine even as he replied.

"The only crawling she'll be doing is in the bedroom tonight."

I couldn't help it—I cackled. Long and loudly, I laughed, attracting every bit of attention in the restaurant. Especially AJ's, who sat there smiling at me with a look of pure adoration in his eyes. So damn sappy…but so was I. Just for him. And I wanted to put that look on his face every day for the rest of our lives.

Charles stormed off without another word, leaving AJ and me alone once more. Well, as alone as we could be in a dining room of hotel guests all staring in our direction. Oh well.

"You are ridiculous." I cupped AJ's cheek, bringing his lips to mine for another kiss. "Thank you for backing me up."

"Thank you for not being a dickbag like your brother." He licked his way between my lips, tangling his tongue with mine briefly. "Thank you for being *you*."

I sighed, pressing my forehead to his. Unable to hold back another second. "And as me, there's one more thing I want you to know. I love you, AJ."

A slow smile spread across his face, one that made my heart race and my blood pound. "Good because I'd feel pretty stupid about this whole situation if it was just a case of unrequited love."

That…wasn't the answer I'd hoped for. But AJ was smiling at me, looking mischievous and adorable. The joker. I smacked his arm. "You couldn't just say it back, could you?"

"Where's the fun in that?" He inched closer, whispering against my lips, "I love you too, pretty girl."

We tried to keep our kisses chaste and public-friendly, but we weren't exactly good at holding back. So when his hand slid up the length of my skirt, I pulled away. No need to get arrested for public indecency when I had a perfectly good bed a few floors up.

"C'mon," I said, grabbing my bag. "Let's go back to my room. We can celebrate before you take me to lunch at the brewery."

"You're so bossy for such a little thing." He pulled

out my chair as I stood, taking advantage of my position to smack me on the ass. Typical.

Not that I didn't love it.

"Bossy? Maybe. I like to be in charge. Besides, I've been craving one of your shandies."

He followed me down the hall, reaching in front of me to press the button when we reached the elevator bank. "Don't think just because I love you that means you get to drink for free."

The doors opened, and I pulled him into the elevator, pressing my hand against his cock as I grinned up at him. "I'm sure we can figure out a payment plan of some kind."

He gasped, staring down at me in what I could only describe as mock horror. "Kennedy Rochester, I'm downright *shocked* by your aggressive behavior." Before I could answer, AJ grabbed me by the waist and spun us, pinning me against the wall with his hips as he nuzzled my neck and made me moan. "But just for future reference, I'd definitely be interested in this proposed payment plan. Maybe we can discuss it tonight at my place, multiple times and in great detail."

I laughed, pulling him closer, grabbing hold of his ass with both hands. I'd happily work off any debt I had to him in any way he saw fit…so long as he kept looking at me as if I hung the stars and the moon. Because that was how I felt about him.

And I was forecasting that particular trend to remain positive over the next several years, if not forever.

EVERY TIME THE front door opened, I looked that way, hoping to see Kennedy walk through the entrance. She'd had some calls to make about the build, so she'd said she'd meet up with me later so we could drive by the lot and check out the progress. It'd been hours, and I'd apparently turned into a goddamn three-year-old on Christmas morning in that time.

The door opened again, and I glanced up, frowning when it wasn't Kennedy.

"Hey, asshole," Luke said, lifting his chin in greeting. "Buy any new plots of land lately you forgot to tell me about?"

Yeah…he'd taken that tidbit of information exactly as well as I'd expected. Fortunately, the plan with Kennedy taking over the majority of the land worked out in the best interest of everyone. There was enough space on the lot for the restaurant footprint and a garden for her to grow her own organic produce, plus an outbuilding in the same style as the restaurant.

Eventually, we'd use the space to house more Pops' Hops tanks, selling the brew exclusively at her restaurant, as well as here. Even Luke hadn't been able to stay pissed with that plan. Especially not after we'd hired the new marketing firm on the island to increase our revenue. With a thirty-three percent rise in only the past six months, we were well on our way to securing enough equity to be able to move forward with the tanks in the projected timeline.

I filled a glass for one of the regulars at the bar, answering Luke the same way I had every time he'd asked me that question. "Not today."

"You're a real fucking comedian," he said as he blew past me behind the bar. "Have you checked the tanks today? And why are you so damn jumpy? You keep looking over at the door every time it opens."

"What? I do not."

Except then the door opened again, and I turned to look. Luke laughed under his breath, but I didn't pay attention to that jackass. Not when Kennedy walked toward me like she'd stepped straight out of a goddamn shampoo commercial, her hair long and loose, the dark strands wavier than usual because she hadn't had time that morning to blow-dry it straight. Maybe because I'd fucked her against the vanity in the bathroom while she'd been trying to get ready.

But, honestly. Who got ready buck-ass naked? I wasn't sure how she thought I could withstand that kind of pressure, because I sure as shit wasn't known for my self-restraint.

"Hey, you," she said, hopping up on a barstool and leaning over the bar top toward me, puckering her lips for a kiss.

Like I'd leave my girl hanging.

"Hey, pretty girl." I cupped her face between my hands and pressed my lips to hers. Except a chaste kiss was never enough to satisfy, so I licked my way into her mouth, groaning when her tongue slid against mine.

"You might want to start charging for a show like this." Luke. That jackass.

I pulled away from Kennedy's smiling lips, her breathy laughter blowing across my mouth. I turned and glared at him. "You're an asshole. Do I do that when Hannah's here?"

"Uh. Yeah. Yeah, you do."

"Hi, Luke," Kennedy said with a wave. "Hannah working tonight?"

"Yeah. She said she'd call you tomorrow before your appointment to do whatever the fuck you're getting done at the salon."

"Wait…you're going to be gone tomorrow?" I groaned. "But, baby, it's my day off."

"Which is why I was sort of hoping…" She

tipped her head toward the exit and lifted her eyebrows.

Oh, hell yes.

I turned to Luke. "Hey, man, remember all those times I watched Pops' so you and Hannah could go fu—"

"Get the hell out of here."

"You're the best. Forget every time I've ever called you an asshole."

I slipped out from behind the bar and met Kennedy around front. She hooked her finger with mine and tugged me along as she led us out of the bar and straight for my car, impatience present in every inch of her body.

"Damn, pretty girl, if you're that anxious to get my cock in you, the seats fold down. And I'm about sixty percent certain no one will walk by."

But instead of taking me up on my offer, she just laughed at me over her shoulder, a few strands of hair blowing across her face. She made me lose my goddamn breath every time she smiled at me like that. I'd turned into one of those poor bastards I used to make fun of. And I loved every second of it.

"Not tonight, handsome. Right now, I want to drive by the site. They finished the roof yesterday and started the stonework on the front already. I want to see it, then you can take me home and have your wicked way with me."

"Orrrr…maybe we could find a secluded area, and I can have my wicked way with you there." I opened the car door for her and helped her in. Then

I leaned into the space, a smile spreading across my mouth. "Again."

She laughed as I shut her door and went around to my side. "You going to wear a hard hat this time?"

"Baby, you know the hard part of me definitely isn't going to be my hat." I pulled out of the Pops' Hops parking lot and headed in the direction of the site.

She smiled at my lame joke, but she was distracted, her leg bouncing as she ran nervous fingers over my hand. "I'm really hoping the stone color is right. I don't want to be too matchy to Pops' Hops, but I want that same feel."

I stilled her restless fingers and linked them with mine, then brought her hand to my mouth for a kiss. "It's going to look perfect. What's the countdown?"

"Thirty-four days until the construction company turns over the building, then another six weeks until the soft opening. I'm not finalizing the official grand opening until the rest of the menu is locked down."

"Everything's going to turn out fine, and the menu will be amazing." I rested our linked hands on the console. "Have you heard anything more from your brothers or your dad?"

Her family's reaction to her news had been a mixed bag. Her dad had tried to get her to come back to the family business, begging her to reconsider. Once he'd realized that wasn't going to happen, he'd relented and genuinely wished her luck on her venture. Her younger brother, Anthony, had been the cheerleader I hadn't expected. To be perfectly honest, I couldn't wait to meet the guy. Anyone who loved and supported my Kennedy as much he did was good people. And Charles…well, Charles was a cockgobblin, and I hated him with every ounce of my being.

She nodded, looking over at me. "Anthony will be here to help set up for the soft opening. He's already working on supplier contracts for the things we can't find locally. Not on Rochester Entertainment time, of course." She shot me a sarcastic smile. "Dad says he'll be here for the grand opening, but Charles… Well, he's Charles. He hasn't even answered the email I sent him. Not that I expected him to."

I grunted. See? Cockgobblin. "Guess we'll have to fill our quota of self-important asshole with someone else."

She laughed, but we were getting close to the site, and I'd done this enough times with her to know just what to expect. She sat up straighter, eyes searching the landscape like she hadn't already memorized every inch of it. "We should be able to see the peak of the roof around the next bend."

I loved that she shared this with me, that I was the one she'd chosen to get to see her like this. To watch her glow on days like today—and to be there to rub her shoulders on bad days like when a supplier didn't come through or she spent fifteen hours working.

As soon as we crested the hill, I slowed and glanced at her. No matter how many times we made this drive, I'd never get sick of seeing that look of pure awe on her face every time her restaurant first came into view.

I squeezed her hand. "Looks like the roof's there…"

"It's the perfect color. And the stone!" She twisted around to look at me, huge grin on her face before she stared out the window once more. "You were right—the gray really works with the darker wood." She gave a little wiggle in her seat, her excitement palpable. "It's really happening."

Probably better to keep it to myself that the only reason I'd suggested that gray was to get her to make a choice already because I'd been impatient to get in her pants.

I pulled to a stop out front, then reached over and guided her chin toward me, tearing her gaze away from the building. "It is. And it's all you."

Gripping my wrists, she leaned over and pressed a soft kiss on my lips, smiling against them. "Thank you for supporting me through all this. I know my hours are crazy, and I also know you're sick of trying thirty different kinds of cheese while I work on the menu, but you never let me down. How do you put up with it all?"

This crazy woman thought *I* put up with *her*? She was out of her mind. If anything, it was the other way around.

"I can't lie…the sex helps." I slid my hand down her neck to her breasts, copping a feel even as she laughed. "Speaking of…"

With a shake of her head, she pulled away and sat

back in her seat. "There's no way we're fucking in this tiny car." She reached over, pressing against my hard cock through my jeans, then shot me a smile. "Take me home, handsome."

She didn't need to ask me twice.

As fast as humanly possible while not getting us killed, I sped us toward my—*our*—house. It was still weird thinking of it like that. Weird and fucking amazing. She'd moved in just a few weeks ago, and several of her boxes still littered the rooms here and there. With as much time as she'd been putting in on the job site and prepping for the opening of her restaurant, that didn't leave a lot of time for unpacking. Especially not when you added in all the time I made her take out of her schedule for daily orgasms. They were good for her health.

Even though I'd been inside her that morning, I couldn't wait another second. I had an insatiable appetite when it came to her, something she didn't seem to mind. Once parked in the garage, I jogged around her side of the car and started tugging her out before she could even get her seat belt unfastened.

"Easy there, cowboy." She unclicked her belt and allowed me to pull her up. "We've got all night."

"If you knew the things I wanted to do to you in that time, your sweet little ass would be hustling into the house."

"Yeah?" She climbed the steps leading to the side door, then turned to face me, resting her hand on my chest. "Like what?"

By the spark in her eyes, I knew exactly what she wanted. A filthy description, leaving out absolutely no detail. Kennedy loved my dirty mouth, and I was quite happy to oblige.

I wrapped my arm around her ass and hauled her against me, then climbed the rest of the steps and led us into the house. "Maybe we'll try some of those toys we bought at Sin. Which one were you most excited about?" I asked, pretending like I couldn't remember. Like that fantasy hadn't been burned in my brain from the moment she'd picked up the item in the store. "That's right…the vibrating plug. How many times do you think you'll come on my cock with that inside you too?"

She moaned and cupped my face, holding me still for her kisses. Her whimpers grew as she wrapped her legs around my hips and ground herself down against my cock. And as much as I wanted to see and feel that plug inside her while I fucked her, I needed her pussy and I needed it now.

I sat her on the kitchen island and reached back to unhook her ankles from the small of my back. "First, though, I need a hit of this pussy. It's been too long since I've had your taste on my tongue." With that, I shoved her skirt up and pulled off her panties, tossing them to the side. Then I dropped to my knees, gripped her ass, and pulled her to the edge of the island.

"You went down on me just last night," she said between panting breaths, her fingers in my hair trying to guide me where she needed my tongue.

"Like I said, too long."

She was already wet, already glistening, and I groaned as I dove forward and licked straight up her slit. Her hips were restless, her moans near constant. My girl was ready to go off, and I'd barely started. "You're already so close, and I just got my mouth on you."

"I've been dreaming of you all day, replaying you fucking me so hard against the vanity. Wanting more of it."

I hummed against her sensitive flesh. This morning had been amazing. I'd gone in to take a shower, and there she'd been—leaning over the counter applying some shit to her face. Naked body on full display, her ass upturned, hard-tipped tits reflected back at me in the mirror. How could I say no to that? It'd taken exactly thirty seconds of fingering her before she'd been wet enough to take me, and then I had. Right there from behind, watching her tits bounce in the mirror, seeing the glazed look in her eyes as she came.

Jesus Christ, I needed inside her.

I doubled down on my efforts, flicking against her clit in fast strokes. Her thighs clenched around my ears, her keening cries growing louder with each second until she broke. Unable to tease her like I normally did, extending her pleasure for so long she usually came again before I stopped, I fumbled with my fly and stood. I'd never quite appreciated the perfect height of the island until the first time I'd fucked her on it.

I lined myself up and thrust inside while she still pulsed from her release, groaning from the feel of her around me. Still not quite used to being inside her bare, even though it'd been months since we'd had that conversation.

"Jesus, you feel fucking perfect." I tugged up her top far enough to get to her tits, then pulled the cup of her bra down and sucked a hard nipple into my mouth. "It's always so fucking perfect."

"You're perfect. *This* is perfect." She moaned louder, her nails digging into the back of my neck. "Oh God, AJ, I'm gonna come again."

I fucked her harder and faster, chasing that release too, so I could fall with her. And when we did, when we both came, our names on each other's lips, I knew she was right.

This was perfect. *We* were perfect, together.

# Trouble is brewing in
# TEMPERANCE FALLS

*The last thing a newly hired dean should be doing is one of his students...*

Dirty flirting with the unbelievably hot barista at Bundt & Grind café is not how Elliott Goodridge should be spending his time. Temperance Falls College hired him to counteract a scandal—not burn through his paychecks on overpriced coffee with a side of impure thoughts.

For the amount of time college student Samantha Monroe spends fantasizing about the new guy in town, she should know more than just his name. But despite putting out all kinds of signs that she's down for, well, putting out, Elliott hasn't made a move. Yet.

By the time the truth is revealed, it's too late to stop the charge between them. Sparks fly, but so do rumors. For Elliott, a day without his hands on Sam is too long—and two orgasm-free weeks until graduation is flat-out impossible.

# Seducing
# HIS STUDENT

# about the author

London Hale is the combined pen name of writing besties Ellis Leigh and Brighton Walsh. Between them, they've published more than thirty books in the contemporary romance, paranormal romance, and romantic suspense genres. Ellis is a *USA Today* bestselling author who loves coffee, thinks green Skittles are the best, and prefers to stay in every weekend. Brighton is multi-published with Berkley, St. Martin's Press, and Carina Press. She hates coffee, thinks green Skittles are the work of the devil, and has never heard of a party she didn't want to attend. Don't ask how they became such good friends or work so well together—they still haven't figured it out themselves.

www.londonhale.com